KINGFISHER TREASURIES

A *wealth of stories to share!*

Ideal for reading aloud with younger children, or for more experienced readers to enjoy independently, **Kingfisher Treasuries** offer a wonderful range of the very best writing for children. Carefully selected by an expert compiler, each collection reflects the real interests and enthusiasms of children. Stories by favourite classic and contemporary authors appear alongside traditional folk tales and fables in a lively mix of writing drawn from many cultures around the world.

Generously illustrated throughout, **Kingfisher Treasuries** guarantee hours of the highest quality entertainment and, by introducing them to new authors, encourage children to further develop their reading tastes.

KINGFISHER
An imprint of Kingfisher Publications Plc
New Penderel House, 283-288 High Holborn
London WC1V 7HZ

First published by Kingfisher 1997
4 6 8 10 9 7 5
4TR/0203/THOM/FR/115IWF

A CIP catalogue record for this book
is available from the British Library

ISBN 0 7534 0136 3

Printed in India

THE
KINGFISHER TREASURY OF
Dragon Stories

CHOSEN BY MARGARET CLARK
ILLUSTRATED BY MARK ROBERTSON

KING*f*ISHER

CONTENTS

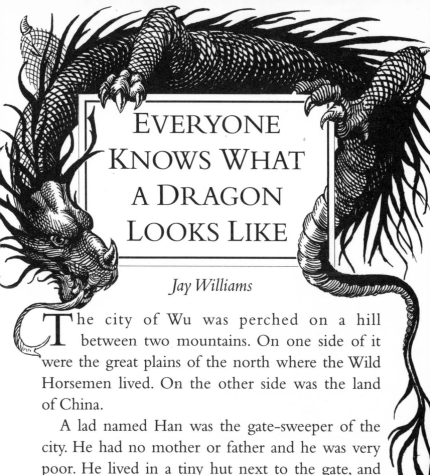

EVERYONE KNOWS WHAT A DRAGON LOOKS LIKE

Jay Williams

The city of Wu was perched on a hill between two mountains. On one side of it were the great plains of the north where the Wild Horsemen lived. On the other side was the land of China.

A lad named Han was the gate-sweeper of the city. He had no mother or father and he was very poor. He lived in a tiny hut next to the gate, and his job was to sweep the road that ran through the gate. For this, he was given one bowl of rice and one cup of wine every day, and that was all he had. But he was cheerful, kind-hearted and friendly, and when he swept the road he whistled. Everyone who went in or out of the city had a merry word from him, for that was all he had to give.

One day, a messenger came racing along the road from the north. He said to Han, "Take me to

the ruler of the city."

Han led him to the palace of the Mandarin, the great lord whose name was Jade Tiger.

The messenger cried, "Beware! The Wild Horsemen of the north are coming, a great army of them. They mean to destroy the city of Wu and bring war into the land of China."

The Mandarin stroked his beard. Then he called together his councillors. They were the Leader of the Merchants, the Captain of the Army, the Wisest of the Wise Men, and the Chief of the Workmen.

"What shall we do?" asked the Mandarin.

"There are four things we can do," answered the Wise Man. "First, we can fight."

"Our army is small," said the Captain. "They know how to shout loudly, how to make threatening leaps, and how to wave their swords in the bravest possible way. But they don't know

8

much about fighting."

"Well, then, secondly we can run away from the city," said the Wise Man.

"If we run into the land of China, the Emperor will cut off our heads," said the Leader of the Merchants.

"Thirdly," said the Wise Man, "we can surrender."

"If we surrender, the Wild Horsemen will cut off our heads," remarked the Chief Workman.

"What is the fourth thing?" asked the Mandarin.

The Wise Man shrugged. "We can pray to the Great Cloud Dragon to help us."

"That seems most practical," said the Mandarin.

So the gongs were beaten, and the smoke of sweet incense rose up while everyone in the city prayed.

The next morning, as Han was sweeping the road under the gate, a small, fat man came walking up the hill. He had a long white beard and a shiny bald head, and he leaned on a long staff.

"Good morning," he said.

Han bowed. "I hope your honourable stomach is happy, sir," he replied, politely.

"Will you take me to the ruler of the city?" said the little fat man.

"I'll take you to him," said Han, "but he is very busy this morning. We are expecting the enemy, and the Mandarin is praying to the Great Cloud Dragon for help."

"I know," said the little man. "I am a dragon."

Han opened his eyes very wide. "You don't look like one," he said.

"How do you know?" asked the little man. "Have you ever seen one?"

"No," said Han. "Now that you mention it, I haven't."

"Well, then?"

"Well, then," said Han, "please come this way, Honourable Dragon."

He led the little fat man to the palace. There sat the Mandarin with his councillors. They had just finished a huge bowl of rice and six dozen duck eggs for breakfast and they were drinking their tea.

The Mandarin looked at the little fat man with a frown.

"Who is this person and why have you brought him here?" he asked Han.

"Sir," said Han, "he is a dragon."

"Don't be ridiculous," said the Mandarin. "He's a fat man who is tracking dirt on my fine carpets. What do you want here, old man?"

10

"I have come to help you," said the little fat man. "But if you want a dragon to help you, you must treat him with courtesy. I have come a long, weary way. Give me something to eat and something to drink and speak to me politely, and I will save the city."

"Now, look here," said the Mandarin. "Everybody knows what dragons look like. They are proud lords of the sky. They wear gold and purple silk. They look like Mandarins."

"How do you know?" asked the little man. "Have you ever seen one?"

"Certainly not," said the Mandarin. "But everyone knows what they look like. Isn't that true, Captain?"

The Captain of the Army sat up straight, brushing grains of rice from his uniform.

"Not at all," said he. "Everyone knows that dragons are fierce and brave, like warriors. The sight of them is like the sound of trumpets. They look like Captains of the Army."

"Nonsense!" interrupted the Leader of the Merchants. "Dragons are rich and splendid. They are as comfortable as a pocketful of money. They look like merchants. Everybody knows that."

The Chief of the Workmen put in, "You are wrong. Everyone knows that dragons are strong and tough. Nothing is too hard for them to do. They look like workmen."

11

The Wisest of the Wise Men pushed his glasses up on his forehead. "The one thing that is known – and indeed I can show it to you in forty-seven books – is that dragons are the wisest of all creatures," he said. "Therefore, they must look like wise men."

At that moment, they heard screams and yells from outside. A messenger came running into the palace.

"My lords," he shouted, "the enemy is coming! The Wild Horsemen are riding across the plain towards the city gates. What shall we do?"

Everyone rushed out to the gate to look. Far away, but coming closer every second, was the dark mass of horsemen. Dust rose high from their horses' hooves and their swords and spears twinkled in the sunlight.

The little fat man stood quietly leaning on his staff. "If you will treat me with courtesy," he said, "I will save the city. Give me something to eat and something to drink and speak to me politely. That

is the only way to get a dragon to help you."

"Piffle and poffle!" cried the Mandarin. "You are not a dragon! Everyone can see that you are only a dusty old wanderer. We have no time to give you free meals or to talk politely. Get out of the way."

And he ran home to the palace and crawled under the bed where he lay shivering.

"My gallant army," commanded the Captain, "follow me!"

He turned and ran to the barracks and all his soldiers followed him. They all hid under their beds and lay there shaking.

The Merchant, the Wise Man, and the Chief of the Workmen fled to their own houses and all the people hurried after them. In a few minutes, the streets were empty except for Han and the little fat old man.

"Well," said Han, "I don't think we have much time. The enemy will be here soon. I don't know whether you are a dragon or not, but if you are

hungry and thirsty, please do me the honour of coming into my humble house."

With a low bow he showed the old man the way into his tiny hut. There, he gave him the bowl of rice and the cup of wine which were all he had.

The old man ate and drank. Then he stood up.

"I don't think much of the people of Wu," he said, "but for your sake I will save the city."

He went out to the gate. The Wild Horsemen were very close. They wore fur caps and the skins of tigers. They shot arrows at the city as they rode hard on their shaggy horses.

The little fat man puffed out his cheeks. He blew a long breath. The sky grew dark and lightning sizzled from the clouds to the earth. A great wind arose. It caught the Wild Horsemen and blew them far and wide. Those who escaped, turned and galloped madly away through the storm.

The sky cleared. The sun shone again. The plain was empty.

The little fat man said, "Now I will show you what a dragon looks like."

He sprang up into the air and his form changed. He grew taller than the tallest tree, taller than the tallest tower. He was the colour of sunset shining through rain. Scales covered him, scattering light. His claws and teeth glittered like diamonds. His eyes were noble like those of a proud horse. He was more beautiful and more frightening than

14

anything Han had ever seen.

He flew high, roaring, and
vanished into the deep sky.
Han gave a long sigh and went to
tell the Mandarin what had happened.

The people of the city crowded around to hear
the tale. They could see for themselves that the
enemy had vanished. They cheered Han, pinned
medals on him, gave him many gold pieces, and
from that day on called him "The Honourable
Defender of the City".

"But best of all," said the Mandarin, "we know
what a dragon looks like. He looks like a small, fat,
bald old man."

TOM'S DRAGON

Kathryn Cave

Tom was an ordinary seven-year-old boy, who had a big sister called Sarah. He also had a friend, a perfectly ordinary dragon.

On Saturday morning, Tom and Sarah went with their parents to do the weekly shopping. As they went round the supermarket, Tom kept his eyes open for food that might interest a dragon. It was very difficult.

Take vegetables, for a start. Tom couldn't convince himself that a dragon with a taste for girls was going to look with much enthusiasm at cabbage or cauliflower. The same went for carrots — however good for the scales. Chips might be better, but how could Tom organize cooking them?

Tom's mother paused in front of the meat counter.

"What shall we get for Sunday lunch?" she asked Tom. Secretly she was amazed at the interest he was taking in choosing food. He was being especially good if you compared him with Sarah, who hated food shopping and had already had to be bribed with a stick of bubblegum to silence her complaints. "Shall we have chicken? Or a shoulder of lamb? Or what about a joint of pork?"

This required serious thought. The sort of meat that a dragon would like would have to taste rather like Sarah. It was a pity that he couldn't see what she looked like inside. Would she be a pale colour like chicken, or a dark brown, like roast lamb? He looked at her with narrowed eyes. At that moment Sarah blew an enormous pink bubble, and then popped it with her tongue, making a noise like a balloon bursting.

If Sarah were an animal, thought Tom, what would she be? Not a chicken, certainly not a lamb . . . . Suddenly the answer came to him.

"Can we have pork for dinner tomorrow?"

he asked his mother.

She bought the pork, and a lot of other things, until the trolley was almost too heavy to push. Tom went on being good for the rest of the trip. He was concentrating on how best to hide some of his Sunday lunch, and thinking how pleased the dragon would be when he tasted the Sarah-substitute.

Sarah went on blowing bubbles and popping them. There's no doubt about it, thought Tom as he watched her, pork was the right thing to choose.

That evening Tom told the dragon that he would be getting another surprise the following day.

"Let me guess," the dragon said, shutting his eyes so tightly that the scales along his forehead buckled and squeaked. "Don't tell me, don't tell me . . ."

"I'm not going to," promised Tom.

The dragon's eyes flew open. "I know. It's a . . . a football."

Tom laughed and said, "No." The eyes snapped shut again.

"Don't tell me, don't tell me . . ."

"I won't."

"It's a . . . firework?"

With his one open eye, the dragon saw Tom shake his head again, smiling.

"You'll never guess."

The dragon sighed and unfurrowed his forehead to fix a pleading gaze on Tom's face. "I give up then. What is it?"

"Wait and see. It's a *surprise*."

"Yes, I know that. But I like to know what my surprises are going to be," the dragon explained. "It helps me get ready for them."

Tom relented a little. "I'll give you a clue, but that's all. It's something nice to eat. Not," he added in a hurry, in case the dragon got the wrong idea, "not what you like best. But something nice."

The dragon looked hard at Tom, out of the corner of his eyes, which is impossible to do if you aren't a dragon, and makes you look extremely strange even if you are. "It wouldn't by any chance be another – what was that thing you gave me to eat the other night? – another sandwich, would it? The nice surprise, I mean."

Tom reassured him. The surprise was going to be much tastier than the sandwich.

That, thought the dragon, would not be difficult. Finding something *less* tasty than the sandwich would be the challenge. Even so, he cheered up. Following his own train of thought, he said in a careless voice, "While we're on the subject of surprises, didn't you once tell me you had a sister?"

Tom knew perfectly well that the dragon knew perfectly well about Sarah, and he gave his friend a look full of suspicion. "What's Sarah got to do with surprises?"

You eat surprises and you eat sisters, thought the dragon, trying hard to look harmless. What could be simpler than that?

He didn't speak out loud, however, because Tom's disapproving gaze made him feel guilty. He could see that it might have been a mistake to introduce the subject of Sarah as he had. He had spoken without thinking, and was sorry for it.

"How was football this afternoon?" It was a lucky question for the dragon to hit on, just as the silence was threatening to turn awkward. Tom's expression brightened.

"Didn't I tell you? We drew, nil-nil, so we get one whole point. Are you sure I didn't tell you about it before?"

"Quite sure," lied the dragon. He much preferred hearing Tom's account of the day's play again to discussing difficult topics such as a dragon's diet and its relation to young female relatives.

Ten minutes passed happily; then just as Tom was showing the dragon the proper way to head a football (using the pillow as an example), a movement above his head brought him to a sudden standstill.

"Ugh. Look up there, Dragon. It's a spider."

The dragon looked. "So it is."

Tom didn't want the dragon to get the wrong idea, so he said at once that he wasn't frightened of spiders.

"Oh no," answered the dragon readily. "Neither am I."

"But – " Tom sat down on the edge of his bed and looked up with narrowed eyes " – but I don't exactly *like* them."

"Some people don't," replied the dragon in a pleasant voice. "Nothing to be ashamed of in not liking them. Lots of people don't."

Tom became even more thoughtful. "If

21

someone, someone who didn't mind spiders, were to put that one out of the window, that would make the whole room sort of feel better. Do you see?"

"I can certainly see your point of view. Who could you get to do it, though?"

"Well . . . I thought maybe *you* could do it for me, Dragon."

The dragon stiffened slightly. "Me?"

"Well, you're not frightened of a little spider, are you? I expect you could sleep in a whole room full of spiders and not give it a second thought. I wish I was a dragon."

There was a short pause. "I'm not *frightened* of spiders," said the dragon, who had turned a little yellow at the mention of a roomful of them. "Not frightened, exactly. No dragon is frightened of spiders. However, some dragons like them and some dragons don't. And *I* am one of the ones that don't," he finished firmly.

"It's nothing to be ashamed of," said Tom, who could see the dragon's position only too well. "I wish the spider would stay still, that's all."

"Yes," said the dragon from underneath the bed.

Tom was too busy keeping an eye on the ceiling even to notice his friend's departure. "I think I'll just go and ask Daddy to get rid of it for us. I wouldn't like it to fall off the ceiling."

"It might hurt itself," agreed the dragon in a

22

muffled voice. "I'll just keep out of the way until the thing's settled."

Outside his bedroom door, Tom bumped into Sarah, who was on her way to the bathroom for a glass of water.

"You're supposed to be asleep," she pointed out.

Tom explained his problem.

"Oh, I'll put it out for you," Sarah said carelessly. "I don't mind spiders. Where is it?"

Tom showed her. "And don't touch it till I'm out of the way."

Sarah gave him a pitying look, and went to fetch the bathroom chair to stand on and a face flannel (which Tom was glad to see wasn't his). She got

into position beneath the spider.

"This is how you do it," she said. "First you put the flannel over your hand, like this. Then, very carefully, so you don't scare him, you put the flannel over the spider and – eeeghh."

The directions ended suddenly as the spider made a rapid dash for the wall, closely pursued by the face flannel, with the result that Sarah and the flannel and the spider all came down in a tangle on the floor.

The spider set off briskly for

the shelter of the shadow under Tom's bed, but Sarah was too quick for it.

"Ah." She pounced, and picked it up by one black leg. "It's really easier without the flannel if you don't mind how they feel. There it goes." The spider went out through the bedroom window.

Sarah turned back to Tom. "Spiders can't hurt you, you know, so it's silly to be a baby about them. That strange noise you made when it tried to run under the bed almost put me off."

"I didn't – " Tom began, but he thought better of it.

When Sarah had gone, he told the dragon it was safe to come out again. It was quite a while before he emerged, and when he did so, Tom looked at him with surprise.

"Are you all right?" If he hadn't known that dragons are green, he would have described his friend at this point as definitely yellow. The voice matched the colouring, weak and shaky.

"Just give me a few minutes. Did you see that spider coming for me? My whole life passed before my eyes in an instant. I almost cried out – "

"You *did* cry out."

"And then everything went dark. Did she – ugh, I can scarcely bear to ask – pick it up?"

"She did." Tom and the dragon looked at each other silently.

"With her bare hands?"

Tom nodded and shuddered at the same time.

"And it's really gone?"

"She dropped it out of the window."

The dragon thought for a while and finally shook his head. "I feel a little weak still, so, if you don't mind, I shall retire early." He looked hard into the gloom of the area beneath the bed. There didn't seem to be anything small and leggy lurking there. He disappeared.

As Tom was falling asleep, the dragon spoke again.

"Is the window tightly shut?"

"Yes," Tom answered without opening his eyes.

"Are you *sure*?"

"I've checked it twice."

"That's all right then," said the dragon. "You can't be too careful with spiders."

Then they both fell asleep.

THE LAIDLY WORM OF SPINDLESTON HEUGH

Retold by Joseph Jacobs

In Bamborough Castle once lived a king who had a fair wife and two children, a son named Childe Wynd and a daughter named Margaret. Childe Wynd went forth to seek his fortune, and soon after he had gone the queen his mother died. The king mourned her long and faithfully, but one day while he was hunting he came across a lady of great beauty, and fell so much in love with her that he determined to marry her. So he sent word home that he was going to bring a new queen to Bamborough Castle.

Princess Margaret was not very glad to hear of her mother's place being taken, but she did her father's bidding, and at the appointed day came down to the castle gate with the keys all ready to hand over to her stepmother. Soon the procession drew near, and the new queen came towards

Princess Margaret, who bowed low and offered her the keys of the castle. She stood there with blushing cheeks and eyes on ground, and said, "O welcome, Father dear, to your halls and bowers, and welcome to you, my new mother, for all that's here is yours," and again she offered the keys. One of the king's knights who had escorted the new queen cried out in admiration, "Surely this Northern princess is the loveliest of her kind." At that the new queen flushed up and cried out, "At least your courtesy might have excepted me," and then she muttered below her breath, "I'll soon put an end to her beauty."

That same night the queen, who was a noted witch, stole down to a lonely dungeon wherein she did her magic and with spells three times three, and with passes nine times nine she cast Princess Margaret under her spell. And this was her spell:

> *I weird ye to be a Laidly Worm,*
> *And borrowed shall ye never be,*
> *Until Childe Wynd, the King's own son*
> *Come to the Heugh and thrice kiss thee;*
> *Until the world comes to an end,*
> *Borrowed shall ye never be.*

So Lady Margaret went to bed a beauteous maiden, and rose up a Laidly Worm. And when her maidens came in to dress her in the morning they found coiled up on the bed a dreadful dragon, which uncoiled itself and came towards them. But they ran away shrieking, and the Laidly Worm crawled and crept, and crept and crawled till it reached the Heugh or rock of the Spindleston round which it coiled itself, and lay there basking with its terrible snout in the air.

Soon the country round about had reason to know of the Laidly Worm of Spindleston Heugh. For hunger drove the monster out from its cave and it used to devour everything it could come across. So at last they went to a mighty warlock and asked him what they should do. Then he consulted his works and familiar, and told them, "The Laidly Worm is really the Princess Margaret and it is hunger that drives her forth to do such deeds. Put aside for her seven cows, and each day as the sun goes down, carry every drop of milk they yield to the stone trough at the foot of the Heugh, and the Laidly Worm will trouble the country no longer. But if ye would that she be returned to her natural shape, and that she who bespelled her be rightly punished, send over the seas for her brother, Childe Wynd."

All was done as the warlock advised; the Laidly Worm lived on the milk of the seven cows, and the country was troubled no longer. But when Childe Wynd heard the news, he swore a mighty oath to rescue his sister and revenge her on her cruel stepmother. And three-and-thirty of his men took the oath with him. Then they set to work and built a long ship, and its keel they made of the rowan tree. And when all was ready, they out with their oars and pulled sheer for Bamborough Keep.

But as they got near the keep the stepmother felt by her magic power that something was being wrought against her, so she summoned her familiar imps and said, "Childe Wynd is coming over the seas; he must never land. Raise storms, or bore the hull, but nohow must he touch the shore." Then the imps went forth to meet Childe Wynd's ship, but when they got near they found they had no power over the ship, for its keel was made of the rowan tree. So back they came to the queen witch, who knew not what to do. She ordered her men-at-arms to resist Childe Wynd if he should land near them, and by her spells she caused the Laidly Worm to wait by the entrance of the harbour.

As the ship came near, the Worm unfolded its coils, and, dipping into the sea, caught hold of the ship of Childe Wynd, and banged it off the shore. Three times Childe Wynd urged his men on to row bravely and strong, but each time the Laidly Worm kept it off the shore. Then Childe Wynd ordered the ship to be put about, and the witch-queen thought he had given up the attempt. But instead of that, he only rounded the next point and landed safe and sound in Buddle Creek, and then,

with sword drawn and bow bent, rushed up, followed by his men, to fight the terrible Worm that had kept him from landing.

But the moment Childe Wynd had landed, the witch-queen's power over the Laidly Worm had gone, and she went back to her bower all alone, not an imp, nor a man-at-arms to help her, for she knew her hour was come. So when Childe Wynd came rushing up to the Laidly Worm it made no attempt to stop him or hurt him, but just as he was going to raise his sword to slay it, the voice of his own sister Margaret came from its jaws, saying,

> "O, quit your sword, unbend your bow,
>   And give me kisses three;
> For though I am a poisonous worm,
>   No harm I'll do to thee."

Childe Wynd stayed his hand, but he did not know what to think if some witchery were not in it. Then said the Laidly Worm again,

> "O, quit your sword, unbend your bow,
>   And give me kisses three;
> If I'm not won ere set of sun,
>   Won never shall I be."

Then Childe Wynd went up to the Laidly Worm and kissed it once; but no change came over it.

Then Childe Wynd kissed it once more; but yet no change came over it. For a third time he kissed the loathsome thing, and with a hiss and a roar the Laidly Worm reared back and before Childe Wynd stood his sister Margaret. He wrapped his cloak about her, and then went up to the castle with her. When he reached the keep, he went off to the witch-queen's bower, and when he saw her, he touched her with a twig of a rowan tree. No sooner had he touched her than she shrivelled up and shrivelled up, till she became a huge ugly toad, with bold staring eyes and a horrible hiss. She croaked and she hissed, and then hopped away down the castle steps, and Childe Wynd took his father's place as king, and they all lived happily afterwards.

But to this day a loathsome toad is seen haunting the neighbourhood of Bamborough Keep, and the wicked witch-queen is that Laidly Toad.

THE HOME-MADE DRAGON

Norman Hunter

Incrediblania was a kingdom, though it didn't sound like one. In fact most people who heard its name for the first time thought it was either an illness or a new kind of dance. But it was a kingdom. A rather small kingdom, certainly, but what it lacked in size, Incrediblania more than made up in completeness.

Except for one thing. Incrediblania hadn't got a dragon.

It had a free sweet shop in the square, where you could have as many good things as you liked, or as many as you could eat, whichever was the greater, all for nothing. It had a fountain that played ginger beer, lemonade and orange crush. It had a State orchard where all the trees grew crystallized fruits. But it hadn't a dragon. Not even a young dragon or even a stuffed dragon or dragon*fly*.

It had schools where every day was a half-holiday. It had theatres where every day there was a different pantomime. But it hadn't a dragon. It had an ornamental King and a decorative Queen. It had three lovely princesses and several fierce duchesses, just as any proper kingdom should have. But no dragon.

"You know, it's really time we had a dragon," said the King one day to his councillors. "Two or three of the neighbouring kingdoms have had dragons for years, and they're beginning to put on airs about them."

"Yes," said the Queen, "only yesterday that impudent young ambassador from Bunceville was saying, 'our dragon this' and 'our dragon that' and 'our dragon, you know', as if having a dragon was the only thing that mattered nowadays."

"They're all jealous of Incrediblania, that's what it is," said the King. "Ever since we started that ginger beer fountain all the other kingdoms have been positively green with envy, and one of them even started a fountain that played water. Water indeed!" The King sniffed, and all the councillors sniffed too, so that it sounded as if they had all got colds.

"Well, and what are we going to do?" asked the Queen. "Can't we send somewhere and order a dragon?"

"But where can we send, my dear?" asked the King.

"Nobody knows where dragons come from," added the Lord Chancellor. "They just arrive, that's all. One day you haven't a dragon and the next day you have. It always happens like that."

"Well, it hasn't happened to Incrediblania yet," grunted the King, "and it's about time it did."

"I know," piped up the Lord High Keeper of Groceries to the Royal Household. "Let's make ourselves a dragon."

"Don't be silly," said the Queen. "You can't make dragons. They're not socks or waistcoats or anything you can knit." Her Majesty was very fond of knitting.

"Pardon, Your Majesty," said the Lord High Keeper of Groceries, who was always very polite. "I thought we might make one out of boxes and things."

"And things?" said the King. "What are they?"

"Oh, just things," said the Lord High Keeper of Groceries. "Barrels and – and things."

"And we could put it up on the hill in the night while it's dark," said the King eagerly, "so that the next morning all the other kingdoms would see it there and say, 'Look, Incrediblania has got a dragon!'"

"Oh, yes!" said the Lord Chancellor. "That would be a great day, would that."

So the next day the Lord High Keeper of Groceries

came down into the market square with cartloads of boxes and barrels and things. And by order of the King every Incrediblanian who could wield a hammer or drive a nail straight was there too.

The King came out on to his balcony and blew a whistle.

And then started such a banging and a sawing and a knocking in of nails and a hitting of thumbs by mistake as you never saw in all your life.

"Pass me the hammer," said the Lord High Keeper of Groceries, with his mouth full of nails.

"After you with the nails," said the Prime Minister, with his mouth full of hammer.

And between the lot of them they worked away so hard and banged away so willingly that by dinner-time the dragon was half-finished.

"What had we better call him?" said the Queen, as she helped herself to some more trifle. She had trifle for dinner every day, did the Queen. She meant to make the most of her reign.

"Call him!" said the King. "You mustn't call a dragon anything, my dear. It's most undignified.

37

You are supposed to live in fear of dragons."

"My only fear of our dragon will be that he may come unstuck in the rain," said the Queen, taking a spoonful of cream all by itself which she had saved till the last.

Then on went the banging again. They nailed boxes and barrels end to end for the dragon's body, and they made him a fearful and fearsome head of wooden planks, with the nails left sticking out. Then the Queen came running up with a simply amazing tail three metres long, made out of goodness knows how many empty cotton reels strung on a piece of cord, which they tacked firmly on to the right place on the wooden dragon.

"Wings," cried the King, and rushed into the palace, where he took two umbrellas belonging to

the Queen's sister-in-law, who was away at the time. And he opened the umbrellas and nailed them on the dragon's back. One of them was a red umbrella and the other a green one.

"How's that for wings?" cried the King, and everyone said it certainly was something like a pair of wings and no mistake.

Then they painted the wooden dragon a frightful terrifying blue and yellow with purple spots. They nailed circles of beetroot on for eyes, five of them. They glued straw round his mouth to look like nasty, creepy whiskers, and they filled his mouth with shiny red stuff which the Queen had saved up from last year's Christmas crackers.

And when they had finished, the home-made dragon of Incrediblania looked such a sight that the Lord Chancellor thought they really ought to charge something to look at him.

"Never mind that," said the King. "Let's get it up to the hilltop. It's quite dark enough now."

So they all hoisted the great, long, wooden dragon on their shoulders and started off, the King walking ahead of the procession and the Queen waving from the balcony. And the three-metre-long tail made of goodness knows how many empty cotton reels threaded on a piece of cord went *rattle-rattle* along the road after them.

They puffed and panted up the hill, and put the dragon down, while the King kept running round making such suggestions as "Tilt his head a little more," and "That foot wants to come forward a bit." At last the home-made dragon was all set up and arranged nice and fiercely, and everyone went home.

The next morning everyone was up early to see what the dragon looked like. And, of course, everyone pretended not to know anything about having made it themselves, and they all rushed about, crying, "Look! the dragon," and "Behold, what has come upon us!" and "Oh, dear, whatever is that?"

And the people from the kingdoms of Bunceville and Spuggatavia and all the other kingdoms came out of their houses and said, "Look, look, Incrediblania has got a dragon!" just as the King had said they would. And it was a great day, was that, as the Lord Chancellor had said. The only pity was that the King and Queen and all the Incrediblanians couldn't hear the other kingdoms talking about their dragon, which was a much bigger and fiercer-looking dragon than any of theirs.

"Now, we mustn't forget to feed the dragon," said the King over breakfast. And he gave orders for food to be carried up the hill to the dragon every morning and fetched back again after dark when nobody could see.

So every morning, as soon as it was light, some of the townsmen took food up to the home-made dragon, blowing trumpets and banging drums to let everyone know that the dragon was being fed. And every night as soon as it was dark they went up and took all the food away again very quietly, so that nobody should know that the dragon couldn't eat.

Then something happened.

One day, soon after they had taken food up to the wooden dragon, what should happen along but a real, live, fierce, smoke-breathing dragon. And when he saw the food you may be sure it didn't take him long to gobble it up. Dragons have absolutely no table manners at all.

Then the real, live, smoke-breathing dragon saw the home-made wooden dragon. But he didn't know it was meant to be a dragon. He thought it was meant to be a nice, comfy kennel for him, so he got inside. It was a bit of a tight fit, but dragons are so wriggly that he managed to get all of him inside and none left over. Then he went to sleep.

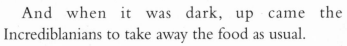

And when it was dark, up came the Incrediblanians to take away the food as usual.

But there wasn't any food left. And just as they got there, the real dragon inside the wooden dragon woke up and saw them.

"Ha," he thought, "here comes supper," and he sat up ready for a good feed.

"Ow!" cried the Incrediblanians, who naturally didn't expect their nice home-made dragon to go sitting up.

Then the dragon saw that they hadn't brought him any supper after all, and that annoyed him. He arched his back, all covered in boxes and barrels. And he lashed his tail. And, of course, his tail was inside the wooden boxes. And at the end of the wooden boxes was the three-metre-long tail of goodness knows how many empty cotton reels threaded on cord. And these came round *swish* and knocked the Incrediblanians all over the place.

"Help!" they yelled. "Help!" And they got up and ran down the hill to the town as fast as they could go.

"Wr-r-r-r-r, brah, crah, rarkk!" roared the dragon, as dragons will. And he chased them down the hill as fast as he could go, which, luckily for the townsmen, wasn't very fast, because being inside the wooden dragon made it rather difficult for the real dragon to get along.

But all the same he came on none too slowly.

42

The townsmen screamed
and yelled, and fell over
themselves down the hill.
And after them came the dragon
with his boxes bumping and his barrels bounding
and all sorts of pretty coloured smoke coming out
of his head wherever there was a crack between the
boards. And behind him trailed the tail that was
three metres long made of goodness knows how
many empty cotton reels all threaded on a piece
of cord.

Clicketty, licketty, rattlety, bangetty, went the reels
down the hill. And they hit against every stone and
bounded and curled into the air with such
twistings and rattlings that no ordinary dragon's tail
could ever have done.

Down into the market square rushed the
Incrediblanians.

"Help!" they yelled. "The dragon's come to life. Danger, take cover. Wow!" And they tore into their houses and bolted the doors.

And the King and Queen came out on to the balcony in alarm.

"Oh, dear me!" cried the King when he saw the wooden dragon all alive and blowing out smoke. "However can that have happened? Call the guards! Turn out the soldiers! Whistle for the police! Go and fetch the fire brigade!" he shouted.

But none of these people were called, or turned out or whistled for, or fetched, because everyone had shut themselves up inside their houses and dared not come out.

And the dragon, after a look round, thought it was a pretty poor sort of place to get landed in for the night. So he just curled his tail round himself and went to sleep in the market square, while everyone else sat up all night, wondering whatever could be done.

The next morning the King got up and sniffed the air.

"Breakfast's early this morning," he said.

"No it isn't," said the Queen.

"But I can smell it cooking," said the King.

But he couldn't smell breakfast cooking at all. What he could smell was something quite different. The dragon had curled his tail round himself when he went to sleep in the market square, but, of course, he couldn't curl round himself the three-metre tail made of goodness knows how many empty cotton reels all threaded on a piece of cord. And when he curled his own tail up, these reels happened to drop in through someone's window and land on the fire, so that they caught alight.

All night long the home-made dragon burned like a bonfire. And in the morning the real dragon inside was roasted right through and done to a turn.

"Hurray!" said everyone. "Now there will be enough cat's meat for all the cats in Incrediblania for a year."

So, of course, Incrediblania no longer had a dragon. But if an Incrediblanian ever met anyone from another kingdom and anything was said about dragons, the Incrediblanian would just put on a lofty air. "Oh, our dragon," he would say, "we had to kill him off, you know. He was getting too old for his job."

And the people from the other kingdoms, who really and truly were frightened of their own dragons and daren't go near them except to feed them, all felt frightfully jealous, and thought Incrediblania must be a very wonderful place.

They were quite right. It was.

A RACE WITH A DRAGON

John Cunliffe

There was once a brave knight who went out to fight a dragon. He had killed so many dragons in his time that there was no fear in his heart as he rode out upon the mountainside to meet the beast. He would finish it off, he thought, and be home in time for dinner. But he was wrong. The dragon was stronger and more ferocious than any he had met before. The battle raged about the mountain all day. Again and again, the knight thrust at the dragon's body with spear and sword. Each time, the dragon's scales turned the blade aside. It seemed to have no weak spot. Again and again, the dragon roared and charged the knight. The knight's horse wheeled and twisted, dodging away at the last moment from the dragon's snapping jaws. Horse and rider grew weary, and as night came on, it seemed as though the dragon must win the battle. The knight's horse stumbled and the knight fell heavily to the ground. The dragon stood over him, and opened its jaws wide, to crunch him up; but the knight called out to the dragon, "Stop, foul beast! You must not eat me yet! It is written in the Rules of Dragon Combat that you must give me a fair chance. My horse and weapons are gone. I cannot fight you. The Dragon Lord himself will punish you, if you eat me now."

The dragon stopped, its mouth still open. The knight's words troubled it and it stepped back a pace. It knew well enough that the Dragon Lord's word had stood as a pact between dragons and men for a thousand years past, but it was hungry, and had hoped to snap up this morsel without argument.

"Oh," it said. "So you know about that do you?"

"Yes, I do," said the knight, "and I claim my right to fair combat."

"But the rules say, if I remember well," said the dragon, wickedly, "that I can make the terms, as you are at my mercy."

"Yes," said the knight. "That is true. Make your terms, sir dragon; I will keep them."

"Very well," said the dragon, "we will have a race."

"A race?" said the knight, going pale.

"A race," said the dragon. "If I win, I may eat you. If you win, you may go free. And the course is once round the world, and back here, beginning at dawn tomorrow."

"What chance is there for me?" said the knight, gazing at the powerful legs and the great folded wings of the dragon. Then, as he looked at the dragon's bony spine, and its long flat tail, he cheered up, and said, "I accept your terms, dragon. I'll meet you at dawn."

"You'd better," said the dragon. "If you don't come, I'll ravage the town that hides you. I'll burn all the houses to the ground, and kill every man, woman, and child in them."

"A knight always keeps his word. I'll be there."

The knight went off among the trees, calling for his horse. The dragon went back to its lair, well pleased with itself.

Next morning, the knight was out before dawn and waiting on the mountain for the dragon. As the sun rose, the dragon came yawning out of its cave.

"Is it you, knight?" it said. For the knight had taken his armour off, for lightness and speed, so looked quite different.

"Yes," said the knight, "I am the one who fought with you yesterday, and I am here now to race you once round the world, as promised."

"Are you ready, then," said the dragon. "When I count three . . ."

"Just a moment," said the knight. "How are we to line up for the start? You are a good twelve metres long, so if I stand nose to nose with you, then you are giving me a twelve-metre start, and that isn't fair to you."

"Pooh, I don't care," said the dragon. "What's a mere twelve metres when we're going all the way round the world? You haven't a chance of winning, anyway. You can have your twelve metres."

"Oh, I insist on absolute fairness," said the knight, "then there can be no argument about the result. I don't want to have to fight you again and I can run faster than you think."

"Oh, very well," said the dragon. "Have it your

own way. Go and stand by my tail, and let's be off."

"One more thing," said the knight.

"What *now?*"

"If I win, you must also promise not to eat people any more, or burn houses down, or trouble the people in any way. Then I will be able to collect half the reward I would have had for killing you."

"Certainly. Certainly," said the dragon. "You'll not live to collect any reward, so it doesn't matter what I promise. Now, are you ready to begin?"

"Yes," said the knight, taking his place by the dragon's tail.

"I cannot see you, are you there, by my tail?"

"Yes, I am here," answered the knight.

"One, two . . . GO!" roared the dragon.

At "two" the knight jumped on to the dragon's flat tail, and held tightly on to its bony knobbles. Off went the dragon, galloping across the countryside. The speed of its going made a great wind that whooshed across its back, and nearly blew the knight from his perch, but he held on with all his strength. The vast tail also swayed up and down as the dragon lolloped along, and it was like riding on some enormous switchback, a nightmare ride over fields and forests, high mountains and wide plains. When they came to a river, the dragon simply jumped across. When they came to the Irish Sea, the dragon spread his wings and flew. Now the ride was smoother and the knight could rest a little. When it landed in Ireland, the dragon paused for breath.

"How are you doing, knight?" it said. "Are you keeping up with me?" And it looked round to see where he was. Quickly, he jumped off the tail, and sat down on the grass.

"Here I am!" he shouted. "I'll just rest while you rest, though I'm not even puffed, as you are. I told you I could run faster than you think."

"But how did you cross the sea?" asked the amazed dragon.

"I swam underwater, like a fish. I was way ahead of you."

"I'll show you," said the dragon. "I can go much faster than that. I was only warming up then. Now we'll *really* race."

Luckily for the knight, this dragon was of a breed not noted for intelligence, and its hide was so thick that it felt nothing as he jumped upon its tail again, just in time, too.

Faster and faster they went and crossed Ireland in a few minutes. Now they faced the wide Atlantic Ocean, but the dragon spread its wings without pausing, and soared high into the sky. Thousands of miles of glittering ocean slipped by below them and still the dragon flew tirelessly on. They reached Newfoundland by eleven o'clock but the dragon didn't land. He went on until the Great Lakes came into view, then he made a long gliding descent, and

landed on the shores of Lake Ontario.
There he had a long, long drink. Then he
looked about him.

"Are you there, knight?" he said, grinning
nastily. "No, I've left him well behind now. I'll have
a good long rest by this cool lake."

"Oh no you won't," said the knight. "I'm still
with you. The race is a draw, so far, sir dragon!"

The dragon groaned and grumbled, but he
got to his feet. He seemed a little tired, now.
The knight jumped on his tail again and off they
went. Across America they galloped – through
Ohio, Indiana, Illinois, Missouri and Kansas. They
rested near Dodge City, then on through
Colorado, Utah and Nevada. At last they came
to California and paused by the vast Pacific

Ocean. The dragon spread his wings again and flew out towards the horizon. They landed in Japan at teatime and the dragon was surprised to find that the knight was still with him. Off across China they went, then north into Russia. Darkness was coming on now, and as they galloped along they saw the lights of villages, towns and cities, gleaming in the blackness. Oh, how they both longed to stop for food and rest. But there is no stopping in such a race, so on and on they went.

"Are you still there?" asked the dragon, as they passed the Caspian Sea.

"Yes!" called the knight, in the dark.

They crossed Poland, Germany, Belgium, and at last they stood by the English Channel, and looked across to England and home.

The dragon barely had the energy to fly across the Channel, and landed on Dover beach, with almost all his strength gone. Slowly, he crawled up the length of England, and came at last to his own mountain. He lay down, and rolled over, panting, on to his back. The knight jumped off just in time to escape being squashed.

"Are you there?" gasped the dragon.

"Yes, I'm here," said the knight, "and I'm not even out of breath."

"You're a great racer," said the dragon, "but you haven't won. It was a draw."

"Agreed," said the knight. "So what's to be done? I haven't lost, so you cannot eat me."

"And I haven't lost, so you cannot keep me to all my promises," the dragon replied.

"I'll tell you what I'll do," said the knight. "If you *will* keep your promise not to trouble the people, then I can collect the reward and I will share it with you. Five hundred gold pieces for you, and five hundred for me. What could be fairer than that?"

"Oh, I'm too tired to argue," groaned the dragon.

"Never again will I challenge anyone to a race around the world. I had no idea it was so far. Still, it would be nice to have five hundred gold pieces. The best dragons always had a hoard of gold and I've never had any. Yes, I agree, knight. Go and collect the gold and I swear to keep all my promises."

So the knight went away and told his story to the mayor of the town, and the mayor gave him the half-reward of one thousand gold pieces, and the knight shared it with the dragon. The dragon loved the shiny golden coins, and spent many a dark winter day counting them and playing with them. As for the knight, he had enough money to keep him in comfort for the rest of his days, so he retired from knighthood, and lived peacefully, growing apples and keeping pigs; never again did he need to face death for reward, on the field of battle, or in combat with dragons and monsters.

If anyone said, "Wouldn't you like to travel and see the world in your old age?" he would say, "I've seen enough travelling to last me all my life. After all, I have been round the world." But he always kept it a secret, how he had been round the world.

SCALES
TAKES OVER

June Counsel

*Scales was a dragon that Sam met on the way to school one day.
Pincher was a Junior boy who preyed on Infants.*

"There was a dragon in the playground yesterday," Class 4 told Miss Green. "Wasn't just Pincher who saw it. We did too. Well, some of us did. Well, one of us did."

"I saw it," said Italian Tina, "a bambino dragon chasing Pincher with fire in its mouth."

"All imagination," said Miss Green, "but it's nice to think of Pincher getting his just desserts for once. He's been a nuisance to us for far too long." She sounded tired and her face looked white and drawn. "Class 4," she said, "I don't know how we're going to do it, but we have got to get our wall picture up by Friday."

"We'll never do it," said Weefy Buffalo. "Today's

Wednesday and we haven't even started."

"I know," said Miss Green. She dragged herself up. "Sam, dear, go and fetch some paper from the bay." It was warm in the bay with the sun shining through the window. Sam knelt by the big chest where the paper was kept and felt heat on his back. "Is she real?" asked Scales in his ear. "She looks like a ghost."

"Of course she's real," said Sam, "but she's got one of her heads, that's why she's so pale."

"How many heads has she got?" asked Scales excitedly. "There's an ogre near us who's got ... "

"Don't be silly," said Sam. "I mean she's got one of her headaches. Miss Green gets very bad headaches."

"All those children in there," went on Scales, "are they real?"

"For goodness' sake," said Sam, "of course they're real, as you'd jolly soon know if you got among them."

He stood up with his arms full of paper. "We've got to get our wall picture up by Friday and it's Wednesday now. Class 5 have got theirs up already."

"So?" said Scales. "What's the fuss? You've got three days."

"The fuss," said Sam, "is that we haven't even thought what to paint yet and it takes days to paint a wall picture."

"Let me do it," said Scales immediately. "I'm brill at painting. Get Miss Green out of the way and I'll paint you a wall picture before you can say Rolf Harris."

"Miss Green," said Sam, "why don't you lie down on the daybed in the bay and shut your eyes? We can stick the paper together for the wall picture. We know how to do it."

"Yes," cried Class 4, clustering round her. "We've done it before. You go and lie down and we'll be very quiet, very QUIET!" they shouted.

"Oh, my goodness," moaned poor Miss Green, putting her hands to her head. "Very well then. You're sensible children. But I shan't be asleep. I shall just have my eyes shut and I shall hear if anyone's being silly."

So Class 4 led her off to the bay and laid her tenderly on the daybed and covered her up with blankets from the Wendy House. Miss Green had made the daybed herself on a woodwork course and it was strong and comfortable.

"Thank you, children," she murmured with her eyes closed. "I shall be all right soon. Oh, what lovely warmth! Like a hot-water bottle! I shan't go to sleep, mind . . . I shall just have my eyes closed . . ."

Her voice trailed off, there was a gentle snore,

and Miss Green was asleep!

"That's fixed her," said Scales briskly. He left off breathing warm air over her and whisked into the classroom, where he hopped up on to her desk.

"I'm Scales," he announced. "I'm going to paint a picture not by numbers but by seconds! Stand back, everybody, and watch!"

Class 4 stared at him with its mouth open, but Weefy Buffalo found words. "Oh no, you aren't," he said. "You may be Sam's dragon, but this is our painting and we're going to do it!"

"I am *not* Sam's dragon," hissed Scales, swelling with rage. "Sam is *my* boy!"

"You're very bossy," said little Tina. "You make much with the mouth, no?"

"Of course I'm bossy," said Scales. "All dragons are bossy. You can't be feeble-minded if you're a dragon."

"Be quiet, Scales," said Sam. "What we've got to decide is not who's going to paint, but what we're going to paint."

"Me!" cried Scales.

"Scales!" cried Class 4.

So there was no argument about that!

"Right," said Scales, stretching himself out full length on the paper. "Now, draw round me!"

It took a lot of drawing to draw round Scales. There were so many ups and downs and ins and outs and curves and wiggles.

"This is complicated," said Weefy Buffalo, as he broke his pencil point trying to steer it between two spines.

"Are you real?" asked Scales, looking up at him. Weefy was a very odd-looking boy.

"I'm real," murmured Weefy Buffalo, bending over him, "question is, are you?"

At last they were done. Scales sprang off the paper. "A-a-h," cried Class 4, "have we done that?" For there before them on the paper lay the most lifelike outline of a dragon.

"One hardly needs teachers," murmured clever Christopher. "One wonders why they don't

become extinct."

"Now then," said Scales quickly, before anyone could butt in, "everyone wearing yellow, do my throat and tummy yellow. Everyone wearing black, paint my eyes and claws black. Everyone wearing red, colour my spines and crest red, and my tongue, of course. Everyone wearing purple – is anyone wearing purple?" ("I'm wearing purple," said little Tina) "– do the purple spike on my tail and the purple tufts above my eyes. Everyone wearing green do my sides and tail green."

"What about us?" called a lot of disgruntled voices. "What do we paint?"

"Dull earthy browns and dreary greys do the background," said Scales loftily. "Rocks, earth and charred trees."

Class 4 dipped their brushes and flew at the paper. Colours glowed like Scales' own colours, battle-red, brassy yellow, plum-purple and polished pepper-green. Scales hopped round exhorting them. "More red, more yellow, more purple, more green. Make me fiercer, make me bigger, make me stupendous."

It was finished. A huge dragon, wings raised, claws extended, jaws gaping, blazed along the paper looking as though it could eat the world. Behind it lay a sombre background of broken rock, scorched earth and blackened trees.

"Terrif!" cried Scales. "I'm a genius."

"You?" cried Class 4. "We did all the work!"

"Children," came a drowsy voice from the bay. "The bell will be going soon. Tidy up now and pack away!"

Class 4 stared at each other. Tidy up! Pack away! Before the bell? Impossible! There was paint on the floor, paint on the walls, paint on the tables and chairs. There was paint on their hands, paint on their clothes, paint on their faces and hair. Never could they clean it up.

"But I can," said Scales, reading their thoughts. "I can clean the whole room before you count ten."

"One, two, three . . ." began Class 4 as Scales

whirled round the room, "four, five, six," nearly twisting their heads off as their eyes followed Scales, "seven, eight, nine . . ." but it was done. Floors, walls, chairs, tables spotless, brushes back in pots, pots back in sink and Scales back on Miss Green's desk, his face glossy with conceit.

The daybed creaked. They could hear Miss Green reaching for her handbag. "But what about us?" said Class 4's eyes to Scales.

"Fret not," said Scales, sliding over. "I'll give you a dragon wash. Stand still, don't squeak." It felt like a hot rough flannel, a gust of warm air, and a scratchy comb. "There," said Scales. He scooted across to the Nature Table and disappeared just as a pink, happy-faced Miss Green came through the archway.

"Children, you have been good. We'll make a start on the picture tomorr . . . good gracious me! Did you do that? You clever, clever children, and not a speck of paint anywhere. I *am* pleased!"

"It's Sam's dragon," said Class 4, proudly.

The Nature Table shook violently and two conkers rolled off.

"Sam's his boy," said Weefy quickly.

"Ah," said Miss Green. "Is he?" She looked hard at the dragon picture. "Well, there's only one word for him. He is . . . stupendous!"

CONSTANTES
AND THE
DRAGON

Retold by Virginia Haviland

nce upon a time there was an old man who had three sons, all of whom were determined to go and learn a trade. So they set forth one day into the uplands in search of work.

When they discovered a field that had not been reaped, they said to each other, "Come, brothers, let us go in and cut the grain. Whoever owns it will pay us for our labour." They set to work, and while they were reaping, the mountains began to tremble, and they saw coming towards them a full-size dragon. Believing the dragon to be the owner of the field, they tried to work even harder.

The dragon came close and said, "Good morrow, my lads."

"Good morrow, master," they answered.

"What are you doing here?" asked the dragon.

"We found this field unharvested, and came in

to cut the grain, for we knew that whoever owns it would pay us for our good labour."

They continued to work, and when they had cut half the grain, the dragon said to the youngest brother, who was called Constantes, "Do you see yonder mountain? There lives my wife. I want you to take this letter to her."

Constantes took the letter. But though he was the youngest, he was a cunning lad, and he decided that he would do well to read the letter before handing it to the dragon's wife. Thus on the way he opened it, and luckily, for he found these words: "The man I send you is to be killed at once. You must put him in the oven to cook, for I want him ready for my dinner when I come home tonight."

Constantes at once tore up this letter and wrote another: "My dear dragoness – When the young man arrives with this letter, I beg you to kill our largest turkey for him. And you must fill a basket with bread loaves, and send him back with this food for the labourers."

Now when the dragon saw Constantes returning, with a donkey heavily laden, he said to himself, "Ah, that fellow is a cleverer rogue than I!"

And to Constantes and his brothers he called out, "Come, friends, let us get through with this field quickly, and go to supper at my house so that I may pay you!"

Quickly they finished the reaping, whereupon

the dragon led them away. Secretly Constantes said to his brothers, "You have four eyes among you, brothers; you must keep wide awake to note where we are going."

That night after dinner, when the dragon and his wife had fallen asleep, Constantes got up and woke his brothers. Then he crept over to the dragoness and took her ring from her finger, gently so that she did not feel it. The brothers ran off and had nearly reached the town when the dragon woke up and looked for them – for he was hungry now and ready to eat them all. At that same moment the dragoness cried out that her ring was missing.

The dragon saw what had happened and sprang to his horse, to go in search of the brothers. He spied them just as they were entering the town, and called out, "Constantes, stop and let me pay you!"

But the brothers replied that they did not want

the pay and went on into the town, paying no heed to the dragon's demand that they come back.

In the town they searched for work and in a short time they were all in business: the eldest as a draper, the second as a carpenter, and Constantes as a tailor.

After a time, the eldest brother became envious of Constantes because he had the ring. He decided on a plan to get rid of him.

He went to the King and said, "Please, Your Majesty, you have many riches in your palace, but if you owned the dragon's diamond coverlet, you would stand alone among the monarchs of the earth."

"But how am I to get it?" asked the King. "Who is clever enough to fetch it for me?"

The brother then answered, "Let Your Majesty issue a proclamation saying that whoever shall fetch the dragon's coverlet, you will make a great and mighty man. You must then summon my youngest brother, who is a tailor, and order him to get it for you. If he refuses, you will threaten to destroy him."

Accordingly the King issued a proclamation. But no one was brave enough to offer to go and fetch the coverlet. So the King had his vizier summon Constantes. He told Constantes that he must go to the dragon's home and steal his diamond coverlet – he would be destroyed if he refused.

What could poor Constantes do? He had no choice but to set out on this mission. As he walked along, he prayed, "May the blessing of my mother and my father stand me in good stead now!"

He journeyed on and soon met an old woman to whom he bade his usual courteous "Good morrow".

"The same to you, my son!" said she. "And whither away? You must know that whoever goes this way never lives to come back."

"The King has sent me to fetch him the dragon's diamond coverlet."

"Alas, my son, you will be lost!"

"But what can I do?"

"You must go back and tell those who sent you to give you three hollow reeds filled with insects.

Then you must return to the dragon's house at night, when he is asleep. You will empty the reeds upon his coverlet. The dragon and his wife will not be able to endure the insects, so they will fling the coverlet over the window ledge and leave it hanging there. Then you must seize it and carry it off as fast as you can, for if the dragon catches you, he will eat you for sure."

The lad did exactly as the old woman told him, and he managed to run off with the coverlet.

When the dragon got up and discovered the coverlet missing, he called to his wife, "Where have you put the coverlet?"

"It's gone!" she cried.

"Ah, wife," said the dragon, "there is no one who can have taken it but Constantes." With that he again rushed to his stable, mounted his fastest horse, and in a short time caught up with Constantes.

"Give me that coverlet!" he demanded. "What trick have you been playing this time, you dog?"

But Constantes only replied, "What I have done thus far is nothing. Just wait for what I shall do to you next."

The dragon could not touch Constantes, for he was now entering the King's territory. Constantes was able to carry the coverlet to the King. The King's reward was an order for two suits of clothes.

After twenty days had passed, the jealous eldest

brother went again to the King and said, "Please, Your Majesty, has Constantes brought you the dragon's diamond coverlet?"

The King answered, "Yes, indeed, and a very fine coverlet it is."

"Ah, Your Majesty, but if you had the horse and the bell that belong to the dragon, you would then have nothing more to desire."

The King could not resist this possibility, so he issued another proclamation. As before, no one dared to answer, so Constantes was summoned to court again.

This time the King commanded, "You must return to the dragon's home to fetch me his special horse and bell. If you do not succeed, I shall kill you."

Now what was poor Constantes to do?

He left the King, pondering how he could obtain the horse and the bell. He knew that the horse would neigh, the bell would ring, and the dragon would waken, to come down and eat him.

What could he do against the King's command? There was nothing for it but to set off as commanded. Fortunately, again he met the old woman.

"Good day," he said, but sadly.

"The same to you, my son, and whither away this time?"

"Don't ask," he said. "The King has ordered me

to bring him the dragon's horse and bell, and if I don't he will kill me."

Again the old woman had a ready answer. "You must go back into town and ask for forty-one wooden plugs, for the bell has forty-one holes to be filled. Then you must hasten to the dragon's den. When you arrive, lose no time in plugging the holes in the bell – be sure you fill every one of them, for if you leave one unstopped, the bell will ring and the dragon will come out to eat you."

With care Constantes did all that the old woman told him to do, so that he was able to get the bell, and then the horse, and to run away with them.

When the dragon woke up, he discovered that his bell and his favourite horse were both missing. Again guessing what had happened, he mounted another horse and caught up with Constantes, close to the King's border.

"You villain," he cried. "Give back my horse and bell, and I will do you no harm."

But Constantes only replied, "What I have done so far is nothing. Just wait for what I shall do to you next."

The dragon ran, but Constantes ran, too, so that the dragon could not catch him. Constantes was able to reach the King and present him with the horse and the bell. The King, in return, ordered two more suits and Constantes went off about his business.

After another twenty days the eldest brother once more went to the King and asked whether Constantes had brought him the horse and the bell.

The King answered that Constantes had done so, and very fine indeed were the dragon's horse and bell.

"Ah, Your Majesty! Now you've got these. But if you had the dragon himself to exhibit, then you could want nothing more."

This idea delighted the King. At once he issued a third proclamation: "Whoever is able to bring me the dragon so that I may show him in public, to him will I give a large kingdom."

Constantes' master soon brought word to him that he was to go and fetch the dragon.

But Constantes answered, "How can I fetch the dragon? He would make an end of me."

But his master said, "You cannot refuse to go."

So Constantes arose and went on his way. And as he tramped along he met the same old woman again, and greeted her with a "Good morrow, mother".

"Good day, my son. Whither away this time?"

"I am ordered to fetch the dragon for the King, and if I don't bring him, the King will kill me.

Do tell me what to do, for this time I am sure I shall lose my life."

The old woman again had a ready answer. "You must not be dismayed, my lad. Go back and tell the King he must provide you with these things: a tattered suit, a hatchet and saw, an awl, ten nails, and four ropes. And when you have received these things, and reached the dragon's property, you must put on the tattered garments and begin to hew down the tree that is outside the dragon's castle. When he hears the noise, he will come out and say, 'Good day to you! What are you labouring at, old man?' 'What do you think, my friend?' you must answer, 'I am working at a coffin for Constantes, who has died. I have been at work all this time and cannot cut the tree down.'"

Constantes repeated this while he got together the necessary tools, and then proceeded to the tree outside the dragon's castle. He began to hew away, and he worked until the dragon heard the noise of his hatchet and came out of his castle.

"What are you doing here, old man?"

"I am working at a coffin for Constantes, who has just died," he replied. "But I cannot cut the tree down."

At this the dragon looked pleased. "Ah, the dog! Well, I shall soon manage it."

When the old man and the dragon together had made the coffin, the old man said to the dragon, "Get in and let us see if it is big enough, for you are the same size as he."

The dragon got into the coffin and lay down, whereupon the old man picked up the coffin lid, to see whether it fitted, and when he had laid it on, quickly nailed it down and tied it tight. He lifted the coffin with the dragon in it on to the horse that he had hidden behind the wall, and away he rode with it.

The dragon of course began to yell out, "Old man, let me out! The coffin fits!"

But the old man answered, "Constantes has got you. He is taking you to the King so that he may exhibit you in public!"

He carried the coffin to the King and said, "Now I have brought you the dragon to exhibit for the enjoyment of Your Majesty and all the people. But I ask that you fetch my eldest brother

74

to open the coffin."

The King did as Constantes asked, and all his people gathered to look at the dragon.

When the eldest brother opened the coffin, the dragon, finding no one near him except the man who opened the lid, swallowed him in one gulp. This indeed was an exhibition — for all the crowd looking in from the casements and balconies of the palace. And it satisfied the King.

THE SECRET IN THE MATCHBOX

Val Willis

B obby Bell had a secret. And the secret was in a matchbox. And the matchbox was lying snug at the bottom of his pocket. Bobby put his hand into his pocket and curled his fingers round the matchbox. He smiled a secret smile.

Bobby took his matchbox to school.

"Do you want to see a secret inside my matchbox?" he asked Jenny Wood.

"No, thank you," said Jenny Wood, tossing her plaits. "I don't like boys and I don't like surprises."

Bobby took his matchbox into school.

"Do you want to see a secret inside my matchbox?" he whispered to Peter Drew in assembly.

"No, thank you," said Peter Drew, who was a good and polite little boy.

During sum time Bobby took out his matchbox.

76

"Do you want to see a secret inside my matchbox?" he whispered to little Helen Wells.

"Yes, please," whispered little Helen Wells, who was a good and polite little girl.

Bobby opened the matchbox and stuck it under little Helen Wells' nose. Helen Wells screamed a loud and long scream. Miss Potts, who was marking books at her desk, stood up.

"Bring that matchbox to me, Bobby Bell," she said.

Bobby snapped the matchbox shut and walked slowly up to Miss Potts' desk.

"Do you want to see what's in my matchbox?" he asked.

"I do not," said Miss Potts. "Just leave it on my desk and get on with your sums."

Bobby walked slowly back to his place.

"She'll be sorry," he muttered to little Helen Wells.

"She'll be sorry," he muttered to Jenny Wood.

"She'll be sorry," he said, poking Peter Drew.

During lunchtime Bobby peeped through the classroom window. The matchbox was still on Miss Potts' desk but it was open.

"Oh, dear," said Bobby, "there's going to be trouble."

The class came in after play and sat down. Bobby hardly dared look at Miss Potts' desk.

"I knew there'd be trouble," he said to anyone who'd listen.

A tiny red and green dragon sat behind a pile of books on Miss Potts' desk. Bobby could see it very clearly but nobody else seemed to have noticed it.

Bobby copied his spellings carefully off the blackboard and kept one eye on the dragon. The dragon moved nearer to Miss Potts and grew a little. Bobby held his breath.

Miss Potts was hearing little Helen Wells read. Suddenly Helen screamed a loud and long scream.

"What is the matter with you today, Helen?" asked Miss Potts.

"Nothing," said Helen, who was a good and polite little girl.

Peter Drew came out to read. The dragon had grown a little larger and was moving towards Peter Drew's reading book. Bobby held his breath.

"Please, Miss Potts," said Peter Drew, who was a good and polite little boy. "I can't read my book because there's a dragon on the page."

"Don't be silly, Peter," said Miss Potts. "I know there's a dragon on your page. Your book is all about dragons. Go and sit down."

Suddenly there was a crash and a whole tin of

pencils fell to the floor.

"Who knocked my pencils over?" said Miss Potts.

Bobby knew. The class was quiet. The dragon sat under the desk and grew a little larger.

"Bobby Bell," said Miss Potts. "Come and pick up these pencils."

Bobby walked slowly out to Miss Potts' desk. He crawled under the desk and started to pick up the pencils.

The dragon was now as big as a cat. It tickled Bobby's face. Bobby laughed.

"Don't be silly, Bobby," said Miss Potts. "Go and sit down."

The dragon was now as big as a dog. It moved to the spare seat next to Jenny Wood and sat down. The whole class held its breath.

Jenny Wood saw the dragon sitting next to her.

"Please, Miss Potts," she said, putting up her hand and tossing her plaits. "There's a dragon sitting next to me and I don't like surprises."

"Get on with your work, Jenny," said Miss Potts without looking up. Jenny glared at the dragon and got on with her work. The dragon was now as big as a donkey. It moved to the back of the class.

"I knew there'd be trouble," said Bobby. A thin plume of smoke curled from the dragon's nostrils. The class watched and held its breath.

The dragon was now as big as a cow. All the plants on the back shelf withered and died.

The dragon grew still more. All the water in the fish tank turned to steam.

"Bobby Bell, open the window," said Miss Potts without looking up. "It's hot in here."

The dragon was now as big as a bear. All the plasticine on the modelling table melted.

The dragon grew still more. The rubbish in the waste bin started to burn.

"There's a funny smell in here," said Miss Potts looking up.

Miss Potts screamed a long and loud scream.

"I knew there'd be trouble," said Bobby Bell to anyone who'd listen.

Miss Potts jumped on to her chair. The dragon moved nearer.

Miss Potts jumped on to her desk. The dragon moved nearer still. It was now the size of an elephant.

"Bobby Bell," screamed Miss Potts, "are you responsible for this dragon?"

"Yes, Miss Potts," said Bobby, walking out to her desk.

"Well don't just stand there," said Miss Potts. "DO something."

Bobby picked the matchbox up off the desk.

"I told you I had a secret," he said, walking towards the dragon. He touched the dragon and it started to shrink.

When it was tiny again, he put it in the matchbox and snapped the matchbox shut. The class and Miss Potts held their breath.

Bobby put the matchbox back in his pocket and curled his fingers round it. He smiled a secret smile.

SAINT SIMEON AND THE DRAGON

Retold by Margaret Clark

A long time ago there was a man called Simeon who lived on top of a pillar. This pillar was about fifteen metres high and only two metres wide. There wasn't much room up there, so all his food and drink (he didn't eat very much) was sent up to him in a basket. He lived like this because he found it easier to think and to pray when he was alone.

Lots of people came to look at him and then he would stand on his pillar and preach to his visitors. He taught them that they should be kind and treat others as they would like to be treated themselves.

Not very far from the pillar there also lived a dragon. He was exceedingly large, with the body of a crocodile, enormous wings, and the tail of a serpent. One day as he was roaming through the countryside, crashing into trees and burning up the grass with his hot breath, the branch of a thorn tree fell into his right eye.

The dragon howled in pain but, no matter how hard he struggled and rubbed his eye, he could not get the thorns out. The creature dragged himself miserably along, half blind, and when he came to the pillar he wrapped his body round the cool stone and laid his head on the ground.

Simeon looked down at the dragon with pity and, at that very moment, the branch of thorns fell out of his eye.

The dragon uncoiled himself and blinked both eyes in sheer relief. Then he went home to his den very quietly and from that day on did no harm to anyone.

JOHN AND THE GREEN DRAGON

Jamila Gavin

John lay in bed asleep. He was dreaming of cars, motorbikes and flying into danger with Batman.

Downstairs his mother, father and two big brothers were busy in the family restaurant. The Hong Kong Chinese Restaurant stood in a row of shops in the high street of a small country town. The neon light flashed on and off all day and night – "TAKE AWAY ... TAKE AWAY ..." People did indeed come to take away a delicious, hot bag of Chinese food and rush home to eat it in front of the television. Other people liked to have a meal out just for a treat, and they would come into the restaurant and sit under the red-tasselled lanterns, leaning over the menu with watering mouths.

It was the night of the Chinese New Year. The swing doors flapped to and fro as steaming dishes were carried through to hungry people. Chicken with sliced almonds, green peppers and special fried rice at Table 26; shark fin soup followed by crispy duck and bamboo shoots at Table 11; spare ribs in black bean sauce, sweet and sour pork, bird's nest soup and beef chop suey all at Table 5 . . . the smells wafted upstairs, but John did not stir. Not so long ago he had had his favourite supper of egg, sausages, baked beans and chips.

Outside, the moon hung like a great lantern. Suddenly a shadow darkened the moonlit sky. John awoke. He could hear a rustling and whirling – like wind; a crackling and sparkling – like fire; a looping and swooping – like waves. Outside his window John saw a green head bobbing up and down – a dragon's head – with red, glowing eyes and a long, flaming tongue darting in and out between huge, spiky, white teeth. The dragon squeezed himself between the open windows. His jagged, green body and long, long tail came trailing inside and coiled itself around the room like a giant kite.

"Hello," said John politely. "Can I help you?"

"I've flown all the way from China," said the Green Dragon. "Over snowy mountains and icy lakes; winding rivers and smoking factories; over vast fields of rice and wheat – and now I'm so hungry I could swallow up your mother's kitchen."

"Oh please don't do that," cried John. "My mother and father are very proud of their kitchen. They say that we cook the best Chinese food outside London. I help too with sorting out the knives, forks and spoons, and our customers call me Hong Kong John."

"Well then, Hong Kong John," said the Green Dragon, "since I am so hungry, and since it is the Chinese New Year, I think I should savour some of your famous food. After all – I am an expert. I have eaten at the finest tables in China – at feasts given by the great emperors themselves!"

"You must be very old if you have eaten with the emperors of China," said John.

"Several hundred – maybe even a thousand," boasted the dragon. "Now then – about this food – I would like to eat deep fried pork with delectable seaweed; braised beef with soya sauce and noodles; bean curd with crab meat; king fried prawns with heavenly vegetables of the four seasons; but to start with I must sharpen my teeth on succulent spare ribs, and I'll finish with a bowl of lychees to sweeten me up. All this must be accompanied with a constant flow of hot, sweet-scented jasmine tea — pots and pots of it. Well? What are you waiting for?" The Green Dragon looked at John impatiently.

"I can't . . . I can't get all *that*!" gasped John.

"Can't you?" The dragon looked downcast. He whisked his tail and ground his teeth. "Well, what can you get me then?" he asked sulkily.

"I might be able to get you something from the set menus," said John. "You know — select a dish from A, B, C, or D — and you get three courses all for one price."

The Green Dragon heaved and rumbled. "I don't care what you get me, anything, but get it fast before I start nibbling your curtains. I am absolutely starving!"

John crept downstairs. He peered through the bamboo screens at the bustling restaurant. His brothers looked like jugglers as they balanced plates and dishes piled high as pagodas, hurrying with orders from table to table. His father was mixing drinks at the bar, while his mother bent over sizzling saucepans in the kitchen behind. John tiptoed to the corner of the kitchen where they prepared the set menus. Taking one or two silver foil boxes he quickly scooped in some fried rice, chicken chop suey, a pancake roll, a few crispy balls of sweet and sour pork and a pineapple fritter. The dragon sucked everything into his mouth — boxes

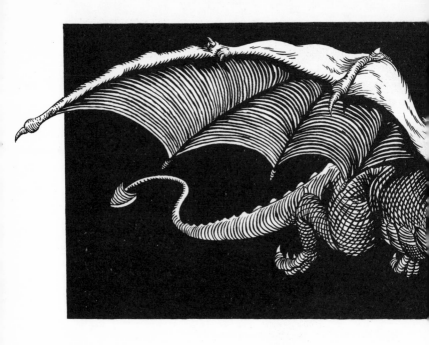

and all! "Where is the tea . . . the tea . . . I must have some tea – I did tell you . . ."

"I really could not manage the tea," said John, hoping that the dragon was not going to make trouble. "I can get lemonade." After gulping down several bottles of lemonade, the dragon licked his lips, stretched till it seemed he would push through the ceiling, then pointed his head towards the window. "Are you ready to go?"

"Ready to go," asked John, puzzled. "Go where?"

"Why, to London of course," said the dragon. "I've come thousands of miles to see the New Year celebrations in . . . what is the name of that place . . . So . . . Ho . . . ?"

"Soho!" cried John, "but that's a hundred miles from here."

"I came from China in only a moment or two, we'll be in London in a jiffy," boasted the dragon. Filled with excitement, John clambered on to the dragon's back and snuggled between his great wings with his arms clasped around his neck. "Which way?" asked the dragon as they rose high into the sky.

"We always go up the motorway," replied John.

The motorway shone below them in the moonlight like a winding silver ribbon. The cars and lorries flitted to and fro like dazzling insects.

The next moment London lay below them — a million scattered lights. They swooped down over the river Thames and followed it up to Westminster. They turned left at Big Ben, up Whitehall, past the Horse Guards, over Trafalgar Square and on up to Piccadilly. Suddenly a rocket sped up into the air showering them with sparks. "I think we've arrived," said the Green Dragon.

John could see a flutter of red flags and fairy lights garlanded across the street from rooftop to rooftop. Clashing cymbals and rattling drums filled the air. Laughing people danced about wearing strange masks, carrying streamers and gaily painted lanterns. A great paper lion wheeled in and out of the crowd, roaring and leaping as children chased and teased it.

"They must have known I was coming!" yelled the dragon. "Look! They've hung the cabbages from their windows for me — I love cabbages."

From almost every window, John could see Chinese cabbages dangling from the ends of string. For a moment the noise and frenzy of the crowd hushed in amazement as the Green Dragon came rushing in among them. Then there was a cheer of joy and everyone burst out laughing and shouting as the dragon zigzagged from window to window gobbling up the cabbages. Children followed, pressing red-dyed melon seeds into

John's hands and tossing red envelopes up to him with gifts inside. All around fireworks sprayed the sky and firecrackers spluttered at their feet.

"It's years since I saw a dragon dance," murmured an elderly Chinese shopkeeper.

As the dance grew wilder, John's arms began to ache. He felt as if he were on a merry-go-round which would not stop. At last he could hold on no longer; his tired fingers loosened and he began to slide off the dragon's back. The dragon rollicked on through the crowd. John slithered to the ground, and before he could look around he was swept away by merrymakers and dancers. He tried to struggle after the Green Dragon, but gradually he found himself carried out of sight – down side streets and up narrow alleys. Just as he was beginning to feel very lost, he felt a hand in his and turned to find a little girl at his side.

"You are the dragon boy, aren't you?" she said.

"Yes, but I've lost him," said John sadly, "and I can't get home without him."

"Oh, don't worry," replied the girl, "he'll find you

when it's time. What is your name?"

"John," said John, "but some people call me Hong Kong John. My Chinese name is Ying-Chai."

"Ying-Chai!" the girl exclaimed. "I like that for it means 'Very Brave' and you must be brave to ride on a dragon's back. My name is Hoi-Au which means 'Seagull'. My English name is Marina."

The children gaily jostled along the streets, chewing on melon seeds and dodging the firecrackers.

"I feel as if I were in China," shouted John.

"Well, people do call this place 'China Town' as there are many Chinese families living round here. Come and visit my house, we are nearly there." They stopped outside a curio shop filled with Chinese statuettes of jade and marble; paintings and ornaments; precious silks and manuscripts.

"This is my father's shop," said Marina. "We live upstairs above the shop."

John followed Marina upstairs and entered a room full of friendly people. They all turned with smiling faces and outstretched hands of welcome to greet them. Marina's mother came forward. "Hello, dragon boy, I am delighted to have you in my home." She bowed, then put a hand on his shoulder and gently sat him down as she could see that he was tired.

"His name is Ying-Chai," Marina told them. Then everyone gathered round him and offered him Chinese sweets – salted, dried apricots, sweet and sour bananas; and there were bowls of prawn crackers and hot tea or lemonade.

John met the rest of Marina's family. "These are my two brothers and sister. We are all at school in the neighbourhood. This is my most respected eldest uncle, Mr Tsin. He owns a restaurant just round the corner. My most honoured grandfather is Mr Leung and he owns a bookshop two streets away." John bowed deeply to Mr Tsin and Mr Leung, and they bowed back to him.

"My family have a restaurant miles out of London in the country," John contributed.

Everyone smiled. The night passed. A sudden swell of sound from the crowd sent everyone running to the window. John saw the Green Dragon being carried along by cheering merry-makers. As they drew near, the dragon called up to the window where John was leaning out anxiously, "It's time to go home now, John!"

John turned to Marina and her family and wished them goodbye. "Thank you for looking after me," he said, "and I hope you will visit me in the country, one day."

The dragon hovered outside the window and

93

John climbed out on to his back.

"Goodbye, John! Goodbye, Ying-Chai, brave dragon boy!" called his friends.

As the dragon turned westwards, the first glow of dawn was beginning to light up the horizon behind them. The last rocket spluttered to the ground, and the lanterns already looked dimmer by the new light of day. John saw no more. The dragon flew back down the motorway with the boy fast asleep between his wings. A few early morning workers, who happened to glance up at the sky, were amazed to see such a high-flying kite with its long, long tail trailing among the pink-streaked clouds.

The next morning John awoke to find his mother by his bed. "Happy New Year, John," she beamed. "Welcome to the Year of the Dragon. Here is a parcel which has come all the way from your uncle in China."

John carefully unwrapped the paper and uncovered a large, flat box. Hardly daring to breathe he lifted the lid. There lay a huge, green, paper kite shaped like a dragon, with red, glowing eyes, a long, flaming tongue between spiky, white teeth.

"I've flown all the way from China . . ." the dragon seemed to be saying, ". . . over snowy mountains and icy lakes; winding rivers and smoking factories . . . vast fields of rice and wheat . . . and . . ."

GEORGIE-ANNA
AND THE
DRAGON

Judy Corbalis

Once upon a time in a far country, there lived a king in a golden palace. The palace had a television in every room, a soda fountain in the kitchen, and in the throne room an ice-cream-making machine that could produce one hundred and forty-seven different-flavoured ice creams. All the waterfalls in the palace gardens were made of lemonade and the mud at the edges was chocolate.

The king had one child, the Princess Georgie-Anna. She had red hair and green eyes and a very hot temper, and she loved playing football and doing daring unusual things, whenever she could find any to do.

The king should have been very happy but he had one serious problem. His kingdom was being terrorized by a huge dragon which had suddenly flown in a year before and had settled in a cave on the top of a hill twenty kilometres from the palace. The king knew the cave very well indeed. He had hidden a collection of jewels there, just in case he should ever need it. And now the dragon had seized the treasure and was guarding it.

"How can I get my jewels back?" sighed the king to his page.

"What Your Majesty needs," said the page, "is a contest to find a prince to kill the dragon and rescue the treasure."

"But that dragon breathes fire," said the king. "No prince will want to fight it."

"Yes," said the page. "Which is why Your Majesty is offering a large reward."

"No, I'm not," said the king.

"Yes, you are," said the page. "Or you'll never get your jewels back."

"What reward do I have to give?" asked the king.

"The hand of the princess in marriage and half your kingdom," said the page.

"HALF MY KINGDOM!" The king was outraged. "That's crazy."

"Sorry," said the page, "but that's what you'll have to do."

"Well, if I've got no choice," said the king, "I'll have to do it. But I don't like it, I can tell you."

"Right," said the page. "I'll go and get the contest organized straightaway."

By nightfall, fourteen knights and three princes

had agreed to enter the contest.

"Prince Blanziflor's going to try, I see," said the king. "I'm pleased about that. His mother's an old friend of mine."

In the next morning's mailbag there were another five entries.

"Good," said the king. "We shall start tomorrow."

And he ordered a large canopy to be put up and invited all the people to watch a display by the princes and knights before they set off.

The following afternoon the dragon-slayers assembled on their horses in the palace yard. From under the canopy a large crowd watched them. In the special royal box in the centre sat Princess Georgie-Anna. She looked at the competitors.

"Yuk," she said to the page. "I hope the dragon gets them all."

"That's a horrible thing to say." The page was shocked.

"Well, I don't want to marry any of *them*," said the princess.

"I don't even think much of their horses."

There was a scuffle at the portcullis. The king peered out.

"Who is it?"

"It's me," gasped a voice. And in, on a large white horse, rode a scruffy-looking prince in a football shirt. A guitar case was strapped to the back of his saddle.

"Prince Blanziflor, Your Majesty," he announced. "I'm sorry I'm late. I got lost."

"Well," said the king, "you're here now, and that's what counts."

"I say," said Prince Blanziflor, looking up. "Is that the princess? She looks nice." He waved.

Princess Georgie-Anna waved back.

"Who's that?" she asked the page.

"Prince Blanziflor," said the page.

"I hope the dragon doesn't eat *him*," said the princess.

The crowd cheered and applauded as the young princes and knights rode up and down the courtyard. Then the king read out the order in which they were going to fight.

"First, Prince Belvedere. Second, the Star Green Knight. Third . . . " He droned on until the princess heard, "Seventeenth, Prince Blanziflor."

"Maybe by then," she thought, "the dragon will be badly wounded and Prince Blanziflor will succeed."

The next day Prince Belvedere set out to fight the dragon.

A messenger returned with unhappy news. "Prince Belvedere has been eaten up."

One after another, four knights and two more princes set out to try their luck.

"Your Majesty," said the page several days later, after the sixteenth competitor had been frizzled up by the dragon's breath, "this has got to stop."

"But *you* said it was a good idea," said the king.

Into the throne room strode Prince Blanziflor. "I'm the next contestant," he told them, bowing to the princess.

"I've got some advice for you," she said. And she whispered in his ear, "If in doubt, give in and run."

Twelve hours later the messenger came back with terrible news.

" Your Majesty, Prince Blanziflor has been taken

prisoner by the dragon. He is being held hostage in its cave."

"How shocking!" cried the king. "We must send another prince to rescue him."

"There were only five more and they've all gone home," said the page. "There's no one left to rescue him. You'll have to go Sire."

"I'd love to go," said the king, "but, sadly, I'm too old. Are you sure there aren't any more princes?"

"None at all," said the page.

They sat together for some time, thinking hard.

The door opened and Princess Georgie-Anna came in.

"Yes, my dear?" said the king.

"I've come to register," said the princess.

"What for?" The king was puzzled.

"Really, Papa!" sighed the princess. "For the dragon-slaying contest, of course. I want to kill the dragon."

"Georgie-Anna!" cried the king. "Don't be so silly. You can't possibly kill the dragon. I've never heard such nonsense."

"I *can* kill the dragon," said the princess. "*And* rescue Prince Blanziflor."

"No, you can't," said the king firmly. "It has to be a prince who slays the dragon."

"It doesn't say so in the rules," said the princess, "and I'm going."

"No one's ever heard of a *princess* fighting a

dragon," said the king.

"They will have after I've done it," said the princess.

The king sighed heavily. "Well," he said, "I don't suppose I can stop you."

"I'll need a longbow, this list of equipment and a red suit of armour," said the princess. "Do you think someone could get them for me by morning, please? Oh, and a banner, of course."

"I'll see to it," said the page.

"Georgie-Anna," said the king, "that dragon is mean and fierce. It's guarding a treasure hoard and it will stop at nothing to keep it. It has Prince Blanziflor imprisoned at the back of its cave. It's already sizzled up the other knights and princes. You can't possibly go and kill it."

"I'm going and that's that," said the princess in a determined voice.

"About your heraldic emblem," asked the page. "What creature would you like emblazoned on your shield? All the knights have an animal or bird or heraldic beast of some kind."

The princess thought for a bit. Then she said, "A gerbil, I think. I like gerbils."

"I'm not sure that a gerbil is quite suitable," said the page.

"Well, it's what I want," answered the princess and off she went to bed.

The princess got up next morning, put on her new red armour, and went down to breakfast. Crowds of people were gathering outside the palace to watch her set off. She collected her equipment and her sandwiches, brushed her teeth very well with her golden toothbrush, kissed the king and went outside.

The people cheered loudly and she gave a gracious wave as she jumped into her red sports car with the golden gerbil emblem on each door and the small golden crown on top. She revved up the motor and set off.

About three kilometres from the dragon's cave she pulled up. She could see smoke on the horizon. "That must be the dragon," she said to herself. "Here I go."

She had not gone far when the smoke began to get thicker and the air felt warmer. The princess smiled as she patted the fire extinguisher strapped to her sword case. "And thank goodness I had special heatproof armour made," she said to herself.

As she approached the hill where the dragon was guarding the cave, she could hear the sounds of a guitar.

"It must be Prince Blanziflor. I expect that's how he passes the time," thought the princess.

At the bottom of the hill she stopped, took a deep breath and marched towards the cave entrance. There was a rumble and a roar! The ground shook. Out of the cave poked a huge dragon's head.

"What do you want?" it growled.

The princess smiled. "I've come sightseeing," she explained.

"Sightseeing!" snarled the dragon. "What do you mean? Sightseeing."

"I've come to see the dragon."

"I *am* the dragon," said the dragon proudly. "I terrify everyone round here. I've frizzled up princes and knights with my hot breath already, and I've got a prince trapped in my cave. As a matter of fact," it went on, "I'm guarding priceless jewels in there."

"Oh no, you're not," said the princess.

"Oh yes, I am," said the dragon, and it spat nastily at her. A long flame shot out of its mouth.

"Could you do that again, please?" asked the princess.

"Why?"

"I just wondered if you could."

"Of course I can," said the dragon, and it shot out another sheet of flame.

"How nice," said the princess. She undid her quiver and took out a long toasting fork and a bag of marshmallows.

"Now, I'll just sit here with my fork and toast marshmallows on your breath, if you don't mind."

"Well, I'm not actually doing anything special right now, so I suppose I could," said the dragon.

They sat there for some time while the princess toasted and ate marshmallows.

"I don't believe you've really got a prince in there," said Princess Georgie-Anna.

The dragon was annoyed. "Of course I have."

"Well, where is he then?"

"I don't let him *out*," said the dragon. "He might run away. He's my hostage. He's playing the guitar in there right now."

"I see," said the princess. "Where exactly is he?"

"Down at the back of the cave."

"Oh."

She took another
marshmallow from her bag, pushed it on to her
fork and held it in front of the dragon.

"Blow again, please."

The dragon was irritated. "Look here," it
rumbled. "I've got better things to do than sit
about all day toasting marshmallows for silly girls."

"I'm not a silly girl," said Princess Georgie-Anna.
"I'm very clever and strong *and* I can tap-dance."

"In full armour? I don't believe it," said the
dragon.

"Of course I can't tap-dance in my *armour*."

"And come to that," went on the dragon, "what
are you doing in full armour anyway? Whoever
heard of anyone sightseeing in armour?"

Princess Georgie-Anna thought quickly. "Well, I
am," she said, "so now you have heard of somebody

doing it. My mother makes me wear armour. I've got a very weak chest and she thinks it will stop me from catching cold."

"She sounds a bit over-protective," said the dragon.

"She is," said the princess hastily. "But, of course, I have to do as she says."

"Quite right too," said the dragon. "People should always do as their mothers tell them."

"Do *you*?" The princess was curious.

"Of course not," said the dragon. "I'm a *dragon*. Dragons don't do as they're told."

The princess was thoughtful. "I see." She put another marshmallow on her fork, then quickly pulled it off and ate it untoasted. "I expect your cave's rather dismal and ugly inside," she said.

The dragon was hurt. "As a matter of fact, it's very pretty," it snapped. "And there's a beautiful collection of jewels in one corner."

The princess knew all about the jewels. She had often heard her father making a fuss about losing them.

"Oh really," she said.

"Don't you want to see them?" asked the dragon.

"No," said the princess. "I'm sure your jewels are very beautiful, but I don't believe you've got as many as you say. I think you're boasting."

The dragon was furious. It roared out a cloud of black smoke and stamped till the ground rumbled.

107

The guitar music inside the cave stopped.

"How dare you?" shouted the dragon. "You stupid girl. I'll show you if I'm boasting or not. Go inside that cave and see if I'm telling the truth. Go on. Look!"

It moved to one side of the entrance.

The princess went carefully forward. It was very gloomy inside the cave. She took a deep breath and stepped past the dragon, into the dark.

At first she could see nothing at all, then, as her eyes got used to the gloom, she noticed a faint glow at the very back of the cave. As she drew nearer, she realized the glow came from an enormous

heap of coloured stones.

"Wow," breathed the princess, "it must be the jewel collection!"

She looked hard. Diamonds, rubies, emeralds, sapphires, turquoises, opals and bars of gold and silver sparkled and gave off a soft warm light.

"Amazing!" exclaimed the princess.

"I know," whispered a voice beside her.

"Prince Blanziflor!" cried the princess. She had forgotten all about him in the excitement of seeing the jewels.

"Ssh, quiet," he hissed. "The dragon has super-acute hearing. Don't let it hear you talking to me. I've been trapped here for ages. Can you get some-one to free me?"

"*I've* come to free you," whispered Princess Georgie-Anna.

"Good heavens, it's Princess Georgie-Anna! But you can't free *me*. You're a girl!"

"I'm a princess actually," said Georgie-Anna huffily, "and if you don't want to be rescued that's fine with me. Just let me know and I'll leave right now."

"Oh no, please." The prince was very sorry. "I don't care who rescues me, as long as I get out of here. All that dragon gives me to eat is porridge. Can you imagine it? Porridge, porridge, porridge, three times a day. It's awful."

"You're lucky the dragon hasn't killed you," said

the princess. "Why doesn't it?"

"It thinks I'm too useful as a hostage," said the prince. "But what can *you* do? The dragon's killed all the princes already."

"I know," said the princess. "But don't worry, I've had an idea. Now you'll have to do as I say." And she whispered something in his ear.

"Yes, I will," said Prince Blanziflor. "But be careful, won't you?"

"No," said the princess. "I won't be careful: I'll be clever. See you later. And don't forget to do exactly what I told you."

"All right," said Prince Blanziflor. "Goodbye."

The princess went out of the cave and stood blinking in the sunlight by the entrance.

"Well?" said the dragon.

"I owe you an apology," said Princess Georgie-Anna. "That's a WONDERFUL collection of jewels – the best I've ever seen."

The dragon looked proud.

"Where did you get them?"

"I found them," it said arrogantly. "All by myself."

"But didn't they belong to someone else?"

"They're mine now," said the dragon.

"But that's stealing."

The dragon was enraged.

"Shut up, shut up!" it shouted. "I won't listen. Stop accusing me." And it stamped and screamed.

The ground rumbled.

"Honestly, you are a baby," said the princess. "Stop it. You're making earthquakes. And I want to tell you something. You've got someone in that cave, did you know?"

"Of course I know. It's a prince. He's my hostage. I told you already."

"Oh yes, so you did," replied the princess. "What do you feed him?"

"Porridge," said the dragon. "It's very good for him."

"Porridge!" The princess was incredulous. "Seriously?"

"Yes. Why not?" The dragon looked puzzled.

"Well, no reason why not," said Princess

Georgie-Anna, "but I, personally, wouldn't waste good porridge on a hostage."

"What do you mean?"

"It seems to me," said the princess slowly, "it's a terrible waste of precious food to give porridge to a hostage. I wouldn't. But I suppose you can afford it with a jewel collection like yours."

"I can't, I can't. I'm terribly poor," moaned the dragon. "It's dreadful. I haven't *any* money at all. And I can't sell my jewels. I thought he wouldn't like porridge and it served him right to be made to eat it."

"Have it your own way, then. I don't care," said the princess.

"But what should I feed him? You must tell me."

"If I had a hostage like that," said the princess, "I certainly wouldn't waste valuable porridge on him. I'd make him eat bacon and eggs every morning, and baked beans and sausages and tomatoes and ham and roast potatoes and ice cream and horrible things like that."

"But I thought he would *like* those sorts of things. I want to make life hard for him."

The princess threw back her head and laughed and laughed.

"You are silly," she cried. "Fancy punishing someone by feeding him porridge. I'll bet he loves porridge, just like I do."

"Right!" said the dragon grimly. "No more

porridge for him! From now on he gets bacon and eggs and baked beans and ice cream."

"Whatever you do, don't give him water either," said the princess. "Make him drink lemonade or something sickly and gassy like that."

"All right," said the dragon. "And thank you. You're a great help."

"I try to be," said Princess Georgie-Anna. "And if I were you, I'd start with the ice cream now. Just watch his face when you give it to him. He'll be really upset."

"Wonderful," said the dragon.

"Well, I'll be off to do some more sightseeing," said the princess cheerily. "Thank you for toasting my marshmallows. Maybe I'll come back and see you tomorrow."

"Yes, do that," said the dragon. "If your mother will let you."

Next morning the princess was back.

"Hello!" she called.

The dragon poked its head out of the cave.

"Oh, it's you."

"I told my mother about your jewel collection," said the princess, "and she thought it didn't sound as big as the treasure the other dragon's got over at Widdock Hill."

"It's bigger and better," screeched the dragon. "How dare you say it's smaller?"

"I'd sort of forgotten it by the time I got home," said the princess, "so maybe I didn't describe it very well to my mother."

"Go inside that cave and look again!" ordered the dragon.

The princess looked worried.

"I don't think I should."

"You must. I'm telling you to," snapped the dragon. "And when you've seen it again you can tell your mother the truth. Why, it's seven times as big as that jewel collection old One-Eye's got at Widdock Hill."

The princess went reluctantly into the cave. Once inside, she slipped to the back and whispered in Prince Blanziflor's ear.

"Did it work?"

The prince nodded. Then he whispered, "The ice cream was *wonderful*."

The princess went back outside. "You're right," she said. "Your jewel collection *is* enormous. I'd forgotten. I'll go home and tell my mother right away."

"Oh, by the way," rumbled the dragon, "thank you for that advice about feeding the hostage. You should have seen his face when I gave him the ice cream. He hated it."

"I'll bet he did," said the princess, and waving goodbye she set off down the hillside.

Next day, Princess Georgie-Anna got up very early. She checked her armour and equipment, slung her longbow on her back and went up the hill. A short distance from the cave she stopped.

"Come out, you stupid old dragon," she shouted. "I'm Princess Georgie-Anna and I've come to fight you and claim back my father's jewels. They're not yours. You stole them."

A blast of flame came pouring out of the cave. The princess pulled down her heatproof vizor and, taking out her sword, she clashed it against a large rock.

"You're not a dragon. You're nothing but a baby."

With a terrible howl the dragon came roaring out.

"It's you!" it shrieked. "You wicked girl! I'll roast you alive."

It exhaled a mighty breath and shot out a double jet of fire. Just as she felt the searing heat over her head, the princess raised her fire extinguisher and pressed the lever.

The dragon's fiery breath vanished. It coughed and choked and spat.

"You won't escape me," it bellowed and, rising on its hind legs with its wings outstretched, it showed its enormous talons. "I'll tear you to pieces!"

"I must be calm and sensible," Georgie-Anna whispered to herself, but her hands shook with fright. Trembling, she took out her catapult, spat on her hands for luck, popped a sharp stone in the sling and pulled it back.

The stone shot through the air and lodged straight in the dragon's forehead between the eyes. The dragon gave an ear-splitting scream. It writhed and tossed and shook, then fell in a heap on to the ground.

Princess Georgie-Anna remembered what her old nanny had told her about dragons. "They're very tricky things, dragons. Never let one fool you. Just when you think they're dead and done for, they jump up and catch you again."

"I'd better be on the safe side," thought the princess.

She fumbled under her armour and, pulling out

a box of matches, took one out and struck it against her knee pads. Georgie-Anna took a dead branch from the ground and set fire to the end. Then she set the branch in her longbow like an arrow and fired it straight into the dragon's chest.

There was a tremendous explosion! A jet of flame shot into the air and covered the dragon. Boom! It frizzled up within a minute.

"Nanny was right then!" murmured the princess. "Dragons *do* have liquid gas instead of blood. How lucky I wasn't standing too close."

Where the dragon had been there was nothing but a heap of soot and ashes. The princess raced up to the cave to tell Prince Blanziflor he was free.

"You can come out," she called. "I've killed the dragon."

"Are you sure?" whispered a frightened voice.

"Positive!"

"But I just heard a most terrible bang."

"I know. It was me exploding the dragon."

The prince peeped out of the doorway and looked at the princess. His lip trembled, he threw his arms round her neck and burst into tears.

Princess Georgie-Anna patted him soothingly.

"Never mind," she said. "It's over now. All we have to do is get back home."

The prince stopped crying and blew his nose.

"Wait," said the princess and she ran into the cave. She came back with a large piece of wood on which she wrote,

PROPERTY OF PRINCESS GEORGIE-ANNA.
KEEP YOUR HANDS OFF!!!

She propped the sign at the cave entrance.

"We can come back later for all the jewels," she said.

The prince took hold of her hand.

"Will you marry me?" asked the princess.

"Of course," said the prince. "I love you, Georgie-Anna."

"I love you too," said the princess. "And when

118

we get home I'm having an octuple double strawberry-peanut-sausage-chocolate-crispy-bacon-vanilla-peach-stardust ice cream with treble flakes from my father's ice-cream machine. I think I deserve it."

"I think you do, too," said Prince Blanziflor.

And he put his arm tenderly round her as they rode away on his horse back to the palace.

RAGNAR SHAGGY-LEGS AND THE DRAGONS

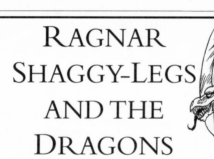

Retold by Roger Lancelyn Green

More than two hundred years after the death of Beowulf there was a king of Sweden called Herodd who, when hunting in the woods one day, caught two baby dragons and brought them back to his hall as playthings for his daughter Thora.

This was a foolish thing to do, and it was not long before Herodd and his people were regretting it bitterly. For the dragons grew at a prodigious rate, and very soon needed the carcass of a whole ox each for a single day's food. And then they broke out of captivity, settled themselves in a cave in the nearby mountains, and began to ravage the countryside, withering it up with their venomous breath. Unlike most dragons these did not breathe fire, but their breath was so poisonous that it shrivelled up all living things.

At this, King Herodd repented of his foolishness in bringing the dragons alive to his court, and proclaimed that whoever killed them should marry his daughter the Princess Thora and be king after him.

Many warriors came to try their strength against the dragons, attracted by the chance of winning fame and the princess. But some fled, and others died from the dragons' venom.

Now Ragnar, prince of Denmark, had fallen in love with Thora; and when he heard about King Herodd's offer, he decided to win both her and the kingdom. So, after much thought, he had a suit of clothes made for him of wool stuffed with hair, and he prepared leggings of goatskin that came up to his waist, sewn with hairy side outwards. Then he set off for Sweden, and as soon as he landed deliberately plunged his whole body into water and then stayed out all night during a hard frost so that his whole strange costume was frozen, like armour made out of ice. Then he tied his sword to his side, lashed his spear to his arm with a thong, and set out for where the dragons were.

Herodd's courtiers came out to see the battle; but when the two dragons appeared and charged the strange figure of Ragnar, all fled, shrieking like frightened little children. Meanwhile the dragons were trying to kill Ragnar, sometimes striking at

him with their mighty tails, and sometimes pouring poison over him from their terrible jaws, until even King Herodd followed his courtiers into hiding.

But Ragnar, trusting in his armour of frozen wool and the hardness of his clothes, foiled the poisonous assaults not only with his weapons, but with his very attire, and, single-handed, in unwearying combat, stood up against the two

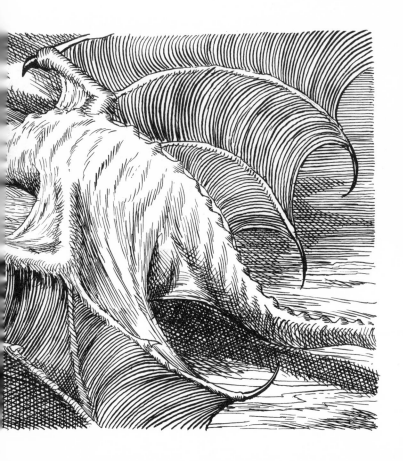

gaping dragons, who stubbornly poured forth their venom upon him. For their teeth he repelled with his shield, their poison with his dress.

At last he hurled his spear and drove it against the bodies of the brutes who were attacking him so hard. His aim was strong and true – for he had waited until the perfect moment – and the spear passed through both their hearts, and they sank down dead, leaving him victor.

By the time King Herodd and his courtiers came out to view the bodies of the dead dragons and congratulate the conqueror, Ragnar's clothes were no longer frozen, and he presented a very strange, shaggy sight – particularly from the waist downwards, where the matted hair of the mountain goats added to his grotesque appearance.

At once King Herodd gave him the nickname of "Shaggy-Legs" in memory of his great battle with the dragons, and Ragnar Lodbrog – Ragnar Shaggy-Legs – was celebrated in song and saga throughout the North.

IRRITATING IRMA

Robin Klein

I rma was very good at climbing. Her parents were calm people, who, if they saw Irma clamber up a church steeple or the outside of a lighthouse, would just murmur admiringly, "Lovely, darling". So when they took a holiday cottage near some steep cliffs and Irma told them she was going looking for eagles, they just said, "Lovely, darling".

Irma began to climb the cliffs and halfway up she found a little door. The door belonged to a dragon who was having a very nice long sleep, and he wasn't a bit pleased to be woken up. He stared at Irma's teeth braces and glasses and he wasn't very impressed. He rumbled like a forge.

"What a cute green lizard!" said Irma.

The dragon, insulted, uttered a huge echoey roar which splintered granite flakes from his cave.

"That's a nasty cough you've got," said Irma.

The dragon eyed her Spiderman T-shirt and torn jeans and the cap that she had got free from a service station. He remembered clearly that maidens usually wore dear little gold crowns and embroidered slippers, and they always squealed when they met him and looked ill at ease. He glared at Irma and spurted forth a long, smoky orange flame.

"No wonder you've got a cough," Irma said. "Smoking's a nasty habit and bad for your health. And this cave certainly is musty and it needs airing."

The dragon made a noise like bacon rashers frying but Irma was busy inspecting everything. "You need a broom for a start," she said. "And maybe a cuckoo clock up there by the door. Tch! Just look at the dust over everything! Tomorrow I'll bring some cleaning equipment and anything else I can think of."

When she left, the dragon set to work, only he didn't do any dusting. He collected boulders and filled up the cave entrance. Bouldered up, and fortressed up, and buttressed up, he smiled grimly to himself and went back to sleep.

Some hours later he woke to a whirring headachy rumbling. Granite chips rattled around his ears, and Irma scrambled in, carrying a bright pneumatic power drill. "Good morning," she called. "There must have been a landslide during the night. But I cleaned it up."

The dragon's scales rattled. Angry little flames flickered in his jaw. He made a noise like a hundred barbecues and he squinted ferociously at Irma.

"Don't frown like that," she ordered, tying on an apron. "You'll end up with ugly worry lines. There's a lot of work to get through this morning. First I'll sweep this gritty sand away, and you could really do with a nice carpet in here, or maybe tiles would be better. If there's one thing I just can't stand, it's disorder."

The dragon sizzled fretfully, but worse was to come. When Irma finished tidying up, she turned her attention to him. She bossily trimmed and lacquered his claws. She polished his scales and lifted up his wings and dusted under them with talcum powder. The dragon blushed but Irma didn't take any notice, because she was busy tying a blue ribbon around his tail. "I've got to be going now," she said. "But I'll be back tomorrow."

The dragon watched her climb down the cliff. "There's only one way to get any peace," he thought. "I'll just have to eat her. Tomorrow. Freckles will taste nasty, and so will ginger hair, but maybe if I shut my eyes and gulp, it won't be so bad." He groaned. Parents, he knew from past

experience, usually came looking for devoured maidens, waving lances and acting very unfriendly.

When Irma arrived next morning, he opened his jaws, without much enthusiasm, ready to eat her, but Irma said, "Look what I brought you!"

She shoved a plate under his nose. On it was a layer cake with strawberry cream filling, iced with chocolate icing and whipped cream, sprinkled with hundreds and thousands, lollies and meringues. The dragon shuddered weakly and felt ill.

"You look as though you're coming down with the flu," said Irma. She took his temperature and spread a blanket over him. The blanket was fluffily pink and edged with satin binding, and the dragon thought it was very babyish. Irma wrapped it around him and fastened it with a kitten brooch. "I'll leave you to get some rest now, you poor old thing," she said.

"You will?" thought the dragon hopefully.

"But I'll drop by first thing tomorrow," said Irma. "It's lucky for you I still have three weeks of my holiday left."

And for three weeks, every day, she came, and the dragon suffered. She decorated his cave with pot plants and cushions, a beanbag chair, posters, a bookcase, calendars, and a dartboard, and she brought along a toothbrush and bullied him into cleaning his teeth.

But at last, one morning, she said, "I've got to go

back to school tomorrow. You'll just have to look after yourself till next summer holidays."

When Irma left, the dragon purred and capered about the cave. "Hooray!" he thought. "Good riddance! No more boring chatter and no more being organized, and best of all, undisturbed sleep!" He curled up and shut his eyes.

But his dreams were fretful, and he got up at daybreak feeling tetchy and cross. He paced his cave and wondered why the silence seemed weary, and the hours bleak and long. He brooded and nibbled at a claw, and crouched in his doorway staring down at the beach, but it was empty, because all the holiday people had gone. Irma had gone.

"Hooray!" he roared. "And she won't be back for many glorious months!"

But why, he wondered glumly, were tears rolling down his cheeks?

Everywhere he looked in his cave he saw things Irma had lugged up the cliff to decorate his cave without permission. "Yuk," said the dragon morosely, and he kicked a pot plant over the cliff. A wave snatched at it, and the dragon gave a roar of anger and slithered down the cliff and grabbed it back. He carried it crossly back to his cave and plonked it down on Irma's bookcase.

"Even when she's not here, she's irritating," he thought. "I should have eaten her and got it over with. And the very next time I see her, irritating Irma will be my next meal! Freckles and all! Just wait!"

And he waited, but all his little flames flickered out one by one, and his scales lost their sparkle, and his ribboned tail drooped listlessly. Winter howled through his cave, and he brooded, and led a horrid, bad-tempered life.

But at last gay umbrellas began to blossom like flowers along the beach, and it was summer. The dragon sharpened his teeth against the rocks and tried to work up an appetite. And the day came when Irma bounced in through his door, and the indignant dragon opened his massive jaws wide.

"Hello!" cried Irma. "I meant to write, but I forgot your address, but just look what I brought you! Suntan lotion, and a yo-yo with a long string so it will reach down to the bottom of the cliff, and a kite with a picture of you on it, and now tell me, did you miss me? I certainly missed *you*!"

The dragon blinked in despair at her tangly plaits and glasses and teeth braces. "She's talkative and tedious and her manners are terrible!" he reminded himself fiercely.

("And yet," he thought, "it's strange, but I rather like her face.")

"Nonsense!" he roared to himself. "She's annoying and bossy and an utter nuisance, and no one invited her here; she just walks in as though she owns the whole cliff!"

("And yet," he thought, "of all the maidens all forlorn, I rather like her best.")

"Didn't you miss me?" demanded Irma.

The dragon began to shake his head indignantly, but try as he could to prevent it, the headshake turned into a nod.

"Then we'll celebrate," said Irma. "What would you like for lunch?"

"Plain scones, please, Irma," said the dragon.

THE DRAGON
ON THE ROOF

Terry Jones

A long time ago in a remote part of China, a dragon once flew down from the mountains and settled on the roof of the house of a rich merchant.

The merchant and his wife and family and servants were, of course, terrified out of their wits. They looked out of the windows and could see the shadows of the dragon's wings stretching out over the ground below them. And when they looked up, they could see his great yellow claws sticking into the roof above them.

"What are we going to do?" cried the merchant's wife.

"Perhaps it'll be gone in the morning," said the merchant. "Let's go to bed and hope."

So they all went to bed and lay there shivering and shaking. And nobody slept a wink all night.

They just lay there listening to the sound of the dragon's leathery wings beating on the walls behind their beds, and the scraping of the dragon's scaly belly on the tiles above their heads.

The next day, the dragon was still there, warming its tail on the chimneypot. And no one in the house dared to stick so much as a finger out of doors.

"We can't go on like this!" cried the merchant's wife. "Sometimes dragons stay like that for a thousand years!"

So once again they waited until nightfall, but this time the merchant and his family and servants crept out of the house as quiet as could be. They could hear the dragon snoring away high above them, and they could feel the warm breeze of his breath blowing down their necks, as they tiptoed across the lawns. By the time they got halfway across, they were so frightened that they all suddenly started to run. They ran out of the gardens and off into the night. And they didn't stop running until they'd reached the great city, where the king of that part of China lived.

The next day, the merchant went to the King's palace. Outside the gates was a huge crowd of beggars and poor people and ragged children, and the rich merchant had to fight his way through them.

"What d'you want?" demanded the palace guard.

"I want to see the King," exclaimed the merchant.

"Buzz off!" said the guard.

"I don't want charity!" replied the merchant. "I'm a rich man!"

"Oh, then in you go!" said the guard.

So the merchant entered the palace, and found the King playing Fiddlesticks with his Lord High Chancellor in the Council Chamber. The merchant fell on his face in front of the King, and cried, "O Great King! Favourite Of His People! Help me! The Jade Dragon has flown down from the Jade Dragon Snow Mountain, and has alighted on my rooftop, O Most Beloved Ruler Of All China!"

The King (who was, in fact, extremely unpopular) paused for a moment in his game and looked at the merchant, and said, "I don't particularly like your hat."

So the merchant, of course, threw his hat out of the window, and said, "O Monarch Esteemed By All His Subjects! Loved By All The World! Please assist me and my wretched family! The Jade Dragon has flown down from the Jade Dragon Snow Mountain, and is, at this very moment, sitting on my rooftop, and refuses to go away!"

The King turned again, and glared at the merchant, and said, "Nor do I much care for your trousers."

So the merchant, naturally, removed his trousers and threw them out of the window.

"Nor," said the King, "do I really approve of

anything you are wearing."

So, of course, the merchant took off all the rest of his clothes, and stood there stark naked in front of the King, feeling very embarrassed.

"*And* throw them out of the window!" said the King.

So the merchant threw them out of the window. At which point, the King burst out into the most unpleasant laughter. "It must be your birthday!" he cried, "because you're wearing your birthday suit!" and he collapsed on the floor helpless with mirth. (You can see why he wasn't a very popular king.)

Finally, however, the King pulled himself together and asked, "Well, what do you want? You can't stand around here stark naked, you know!"

"Your Majesty!" cried the merchant. "The Jade Dragon has flown down from the Jade Dragon Snow Mountain and is sitting on my rooftop!"

The King went a little green about the gills when he heard this, because nobody particularly likes having a dragon in their kingdom.

"Well, what do you expect me to do about it?" replied the King. "Go and read it a bedtime story?"

"Oh no! Most Cherished Lord! Admired And Venerated Leader Of His People! No one would expect *you* to read bedtime stories to a dragon. But I was hoping you might find some way of . . . getting rid of it?"

"Is it a big dragon?" asked the King.

"It is. Very big," replied the merchant.

"I was afraid it would be," said the King. "And have you tried asking it – politely – if it would mind leaving of its own accord?"

"First thing we did," said the merchant.

"Well, in that case," replied the King, ". . . tough luck!"

Just at that moment there was a terrible noise from outside the palace. "Ah! It's here!" cried the King, leaping on to a chair. "The dragon's come to get us!"

"No, no, no," said the Lord High Chancellor. "That is nothing to be worried about. It is merely the poor people of your kingdom groaning at your gates, because they have not enough to eat."

"Miserable wretches!" cried the King. "Have them all beaten and sent home."

"Er . . . many of them have no homes to go to," replied the Chancellor.

"Well then – obviously – just have them beaten!" exclaimed the King. "And sent somewhere else to groan."

But just then there was an even louder roar from outside the palace gates.

"*That's* the dragon!" exclaimed the King, hiding in a cupboard.

"No," said the Chancellor, "that is merely the

rest of your subjects demanding that you resign the crown."

At this point, the King sat on his throne and burst into tears. "Why does nobody like me?" he cried.

"Er . . . may I go and put some clothes on?" asked the merchant.

"Oh! Go and jump out of the window!" replied the King.

Well, the merchant was just going to jump out of the window (because, of course, in those days, whenever a king told you to do something, you always did it) when the Lord High Chancellor stopped him and turned to the King and whispered, "Your Majesty! It may be that this fellow's dragon could be just what we need!"

"Don't talk piffle," snapped the King. "*Nobody* needs a dragon!"

"On the contrary," replied the Chancellor, "*you* need one right now. Nothing, you know, makes a king more popular with his people than getting rid of a dragon for them."

"You're right!" exclaimed the King.

So there and then he sent for the Most Famous Dragon-Slayer In The Land, and had it announced that a terrible dragon had flown down from the Jade Dragon Snow Mountain and was threatening their kingdom.

Naturally everyone immediately forgot about being hungry or discontented. They fled from the palace gates and hid themselves away in dark corners for fear of the dragon.

Some days later, the Most Famous Dragon-Slayer In The Whole Of China arrived. The King ordered a fabulous banquet in his honour. But the Dragon-Slayer said, "I never eat so much as a nut, nor drink so much as a thimbleful, until I have seen my dragon, and know what it is I have to do."

So the merchant took the Dragon-Slayer to his house, and they hid in an apricot tree to observe the dragon.

"Well? What d'you think of it?" asked the merchant.

But the Dragon-Slayer said not a word.

"Big, isn't it?" said the merchant.

But the Dragon-Slayer remained silent. He just sat there in the apricot tree, watching the dragon.

"How are you going to kill it?" inquired the merchant eagerly.

But the Dragon-Slayer didn't reply. He climbed

down out of the apricot tree, and returned to the palace. There he ordered a plate of eels and mint, and he drank a cup of wine.

When he had finished, the King looked at him anxiously and said, "Well? What are you going to do?"

The Dragon-Slayer wiped his mouth and said, "Nothing."

"Nothing?" exclaimed the King. "Is this dragon so big you're frightened of it?"

"I've killed bigger ones," replied the Dragon-Slayer, rubbing his chest.

"Is it such a fierce dragon you're scared it'll finish you off?" cried the King.

"I've dispatched hundreds of fiercer ones," yawned the Dragon-Slayer.

"Then has it hotter breath?" demanded the King. "Or sharper claws? Or bigger jaws? Or what?"

But the Dragon-Slayer merely shut his eyes and said, "Like me, it's old and tired. It has come down from the mountains to die in the East. It's merely resting on that rooftop. It'll do no harm, and, in a week or so, it will go on its way to the place where dragons go to die."

Then the Dragon-Slayer rolled himself up in his cloak and went to sleep by the fire.

But the King was furious.

"This is no good!" he whispered to the Lord High Chancellor. "It's not going to make me more popular if I leave this dragon sitting on that man's rooftop. It needs to be killed!"

"I agree," replied the Lord High Chancellor. "There's nothing like a little dragon-slaying to get the people on to your side."

So the King sent for the Second Most Famous Dragon-Slayer In The Whole Of China, and said, "Listen! I want you to kill that dragon, and I won't pay you unless you do!"

So the Second Most Famous Dragon-Slayer In The Whole Of China went to the merchant's house and hid in the apricot tree to observe the dragon. Then he came back to the palace, and ordered a plate of pork and beans, drank a flask of wine, and said to the King, "It's a messy business killing dragons. The fire from their nostrils burns the countryside, and their blood poisons the land so that nothing will grow for a hundred years. And when you cut them open, the smoke from their bellies covers the sky and blots out the sun."

But the King said, "I want that dragon killed. Mess or no mess!"

But the Second Most Famous Dragon-Slayer In The Whole Of China replied, "Best to leave this one alone. It's old and on its way to die in the East."

Whereupon the King stamped his foot, and sent for the Third Most Famous Dragon-Slayer In The Whole Of China, and said, "Kill me that dragon!"

Now the Third Most Famous Dragon-Slayer In The Whole Of China also happened to be the most cunning, and he knew just why it was the King was so keen to have the dragon killed. He also knew that if he killed the dragon, he himself would become the First Dragon-Slayer In The Whole Of China instead of only the Third. So he said to the King, "Nothing easier, Your Majesty. I'll kill that dragon straightaway."

Well, he went to the merchant's house, climbed the apricot tree and looked down at the dragon. He could see it was an old one and weary of life, and he congratulated himself on his good luck. But he told the King to have it announced in the market square that the dragon was young and fierce and very dangerous, and that everyone should keep well out of the way until after the battle was over.

When they heard this, of course, the people were even more frightened, and they hurried back to their hiding-places and shut their windows and bolted their doors.

Then the Dragon-Slayer shouted down from the apricot tree, "Wake up, Jade Dragon! For I have come to kill you!"

The Jade Dragon opened a weary eye and said, "Leave me alone, Dragon-Slayer. I am old and weary of life. I have come down from the Jade Dragon Snow Mountain to die in the East. Why should you kill me?"

"Enough!" cried the Dragon-Slayer. "If you do not want me to kill you, fly away and never come back."

The Jade Dragon opened its other weary eye and looked at the Dragon-Slayer. "Dragon-Slayer! You know I am too weary to fly any further. I have settled here to rest. I shall do no one any harm. Let me be."

But the Dragon-Slayer didn't reply. He took his bow and he took two arrows, and he let one arrow fly, and it pierced the Jade Dragon in the right eye. The old creature roared in pain, and tried to raise itself up on its legs, but it was too old and weak, and it fell down again on top of the house, crushing one of the walls beneath its weight.

Then the Dragon-Slayer fired his second arrow, and it pierced the Jade Dragon in the left eye, and the old creature roared again and a sheet of fire shot out from its nostrils and set fire to the apricot tree.

But the Dragon-Slayer had leapt out of the tree
and on to the back of the blinded beast, as it
struggled to its feet, breathing flames through its
nostrils and setting fire to the countryside all
around.

It flapped its old, leathery wings, trying to fly

away, but the Dragon-Slayer was hanging on to the spines on its back, and he drove his long sword deep into the dragon's side. And the Jade Dragon howled, and its claws ripped off the roof of the merchant's house, as it rolled over on to its side and its blood gushed out on to the ground.

And everywhere the dragon's blood touched the earth, the plants turned black and withered away.

Then the Dragon-Slayer took his long sword and cut open the old dragon's fiery belly, and a black cloud shot up into the sky and covered the sun.

When the people looked out of their hiding places, they thought the night had fallen, the sky was so black. All around the city they could see the countryside burning, and the air stank with the smell of the dragon's blood. But the King ordered a great banquet to be held in the palace that night, and he paid the Dragon-Slayer half the money he had in his treasury.

And when the people heard that the dragon had been killed, they cheered and clapped and praised the King because he had saved them from the dragon.

When the merchant and his wife and children returned to their house, however, they found it was just a pile of rubble, and their beautiful lawns and gardens were burnt beyond repair.

And the sun did not shine again in that land all that summer, because of the smoke from the dragon's belly. What is worse, nothing would grow in that kingdom for a hundred years, because the land had been poisoned by the dragon's blood.

But the odd thing is, that although the people were now poorer than they ever had been, and scarcely ever had enough to eat or saw the sun, every time the King went out they cheered him and clapped him and called him, "King Chong The Dragon-Slayer," and he was, from that time on, the most popular ruler in the whole of China for as long as he reigned and long after.

And the Third Most Famous Dragon-Slayer In The Whole Of China became the First, and people never tired of telling and retelling the story of his fearful fight with the Jade Dragon from the Jade Dragon Snow Mountain.

What do you think of that?

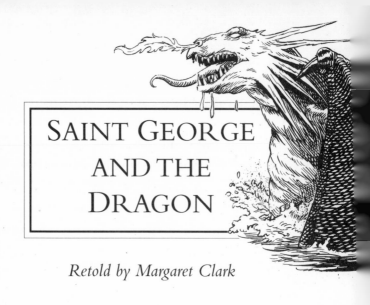

SAINT GEORGE AND THE DRAGON

Retold by Margaret Clark

L ong, long ago there was a city whose inhabitants lived in constant fear of a dragon. This dragon had wings as big as a ship's sails and when it flew it cast a gigantic shadow that terrorized everyone in its path. In its gaping mouth were three rows of iron teeth, and its eyes blazed like two bright suns.

No one knew where the dragon had come from. One morning the people of the city had been woken by a noise like a roll of thunder and when they rushed out of their houses to see what had happened they found flocks of birds screeching and squawking and flying in all directions, while their animals – cows, sheep and goats – were running in terror from the pasture by the lake.

After that day the citizens kept their animals safe within the city walls and bolted the city gates.

150

The dragon spent most of its time sleeping in the murky depths of the lake not far from the city walls, but at dusk it would heave its great body out of the water and lumber off in search of food. It ate every living thing it could find and with the flames that roared from its mouth it charred every tree and blade of grass for miles around. Then in its fury the dragon came right up to the city walls and breathed fire and poison into the streets so that all the men, women and children, with the cows, the sheep and the goats, had to shelter wherever they could to escape the heat and the stench of its breath.

"What are we to do?" said the king, who was the most frightened of them all. "Who is brave enough to go out and fight this dragon?" When no one answered him, he groaned. "Then if we cannot kill the dragon, we must try to keep it away from our city by leaving food for it near its sleeping place in the lake."

So they began by dragging two sheep to the lake, where they tethered the animals to a tree-trunk while the dragon slept. That night it did not come near the city and the citizens felt safe in their beds. They did this until there were no more sheep left. Then they took the cows and the goats, and even the cats and the dogs to the dragon, but still its hunger was not satisfied.

At last they realized there was nothing more to offer to the dragon except themselves. But who should be the first? They decided to draw lots. They collected all the small white pebbles they could find and put them in a bag with just one black stone. They tied a string round the top of the bag and pulled it tight until there was only room to put in a hand. Then each citizen in turn, as well as the king and his daughter, picked out a stone. Whoever got the black one was taken out to the dragon's lair so that the rest could live in safety and at peace.

Every day there was much weeping as children lost their fathers, mothers lost their sons and babies

lost their grandparents. Then one morning it was the king's daughter who found the black stone in the palm of her hand. The king shouted out in his grief. He loved her so much that he told the people he would give them all his gold and silver in return for her life. But they said, "No, why should she be spared when so many of *our* children have been sacrificed?"

The princess herself was a good girl and although she was very frightened she knew that her father must share the suffering of his people. So when the king kissed her and said goodbye, she held her head up bravely as she was led out of the city to the dragon's lair. She never looked back and did not flinch as she was bound with ropes to the tree-trunk. But when she was left alone to wait for the moment when the dragon would wake up, she began to cry very quietly.

Then she heard a sudden noise – the sound of a horse's hooves – and across the charred ground came a knight. His horse was pure white, his shield bore a red cross, and his armour was so highly polished that it glittered in the setting sun.

"Why are you weeping?" asked the knight.

"Oh, don't stop," answered the princess. "Go on your way quickly or you will surely die, as I shall, very soon."

"Why are you going to die?" said the knight, and when the princess told him about the dragon he drew his sword from its scabbard and held it above his head. "Don't be afraid," he said. "By the vows I took when I became a knight, I promised to help anyone in distress and to fight evil wherever I find it. Trust me! I shall fight the dragon and I shall win."

Immediately there was a stirring in the lake as the dragon began to haul itself out of the water. The knight's horse reared in terror as the dragon opened its hideous mouth and roaring flames appeared. But the knight swung his sword against the dragon's wing and when it lifted the wing in pain the knight flung himself against the dragon's body and plunged his sword into its side. The dragon fell to the ground and the knight swiftly freed the princess from the ropes that held her. "Give me your girdle," he said, "and I will bind it round the dragon's neck."

And when he did this, the dragon closed its
cruel jaws, picked up its feet and followed the
princess and the knight meekly into the city. The
people looked out of their windows and could not
believe their eyes. Then the king saw his daughter
and rushed to embrace her, shouting for joy that
she was alive.

When at last the people dared to creep out of their homes, the knight cut off the dragon's head so that they all knew it was dead and they could live at peace once more. They threw the dragon's body into the lake where it sank and was never seen again. Gradually the grass and trees began to grow and the people returned to enjoying life as they had done before.

The king offered the knight a reward of many gold pieces but the knight would have none of it and asked that it should be given to the poor. Then he left the city and rode away in search of more adventure.

The name of this good knight was George and he became the patron saint of England, being renowned for his courage and devotion. St George's Day is celebrated each year on 23 April, when a feast is given for members of the Order of the Garter, the highest order of knighthood, founded in 1348 by King Edward III, in honour of St George.

Acknowledgements

The publisher would like to thank the copyright holders for permission to reproduce the following copyright material:

Kathryn Cave: Penguin Books for Chapter Seven from *Dragonrise* by Kathryn Cave, Penguin Books 1984. Copyright © Kathryn Cave 1984. **Margaret Clark:** the author for "Saint George and the Dragon" and "Saint Simeon and the Dragon". Copyright © Margaret Clark 1997. **Judy Corbalis**: Scholastic Children's Books for "Georgie-Anna and the Dragon" taken from *The Wrestling Princess and Other Stories* by Judy Corbalis, Scholastic 1986. Text copyright © Judy Corbalis 1986. **June Counsel**: Faber and Faber Ltd for "Scales Takes Over" from *A Dragon in Class 4* by June Counsel, Faber and Faber Ltd 1984. Copyright © June Counsel 1984. **John Cunliffe**: Scholastic Children's Books for "A Race With a Dragon" taken from *The Great Dragon Competition and Other Stories* by John Cunliffe, Scholastic 1973. Text copyright © John Cunliffe 1973. **Jamila Gavin**: Reed Consumer Books Ltd for "John and the Green Dragon" from *The Magic Orange Tree and Other Stories* by Jamila Gavin, Methuen Children's Books 1979. Copyright © Jamila Gavin 1979. **Roger Lancelyn Green**: Penguin Books for "Ragnar Shaggy-Legs and the Dragons" from *A Book of Dragons* edited by Roger Lancelyn Green, Hamish Hamilton 1970. Copyright © Roger Lancelyn Green 1970. **Virginia Haviland**: Little, Brown and Company for "Constantes and the Dragon" from *Favourite Fairy Tales Told Around the World* by Virginia Haviland. Text copyright © 1985 Virginia Haviland; illustrations copyright © 1985 S D Schindler. **Norman Hunter**: Random House UK for "The Home-made Dragon" from *The Home-made Dragon and Other Incredible Stories* by Norman Hunter, The Bodley Head 1971. Copyright © Norman Hunter 1971. **Terry Jones**: Pavilion Books for "The Dragon on the Roof" from *Fantastic Stories* by Terry Jones, Pavilion Books 1992. Copyright © Terry Jones 1992. **Robin Klein**: Curtis Brown, London for "Irritating Irma" by Robin Klein. Copyright © Robin Klein 1980. **Jay Williams**: Mrs Barbara Williams for "Everyone Knows What a Dragon Looks Like" by Jay Williams, Four Winds Press 1976. Copyright © Jay Williams 1976. **Val Willis**: Scholastic Children's Books for "The Secret in the Matchbox" by Val Willis, Scholastic 1988. Text copyright © Val Willis 1988.

Every effort has been made to obtain permission to reproduce copyright material but there may be cases where we have been unable to trace a copyright holder. The publisher will be happy to correct any omissions in future printings.

Titles in the
Kingfisher Treasury series